Elizabeth kn she couldn't fight me-thing . . . may e a good story. . . . wly, "you've never h vith steroids or students having to—"

"God, Liz," Ken said with a soft laugh. "What do you think this is? A *7th Heaven* episode?"

"Oh, yeah." Jessica grinned. "Liz really identifies with that show. She's so into Matt."

Elizabeth glared at Jessica. "So anyway, Ken—"

But Ken suddenly looked at his watch. "Sorry, Liz, gotta run." He picked up his tray and his backpack and stood up from the table. Maria stood too, but Ken gave her a quick peck on the lips. "Call you tonight," he said. Then he was gone.

They all looked at Maria, who slowly sank back down in her chair.

"Hey," Elizabeth said, "sorry if I said something wrong, Maria."

Maria shrugged. "It's okay. You know how those teams are—they have their code of honor and all that."

Elizabeth smiled at her but couldn't help wondering how she could stand such a touchy boyfriend. Conner had been touchy too—well, that was an understatement. Elizabeth was so glad not to have to deal with that kind of thing anymore. She had to admit her new attitude was a nice change. She only had to worry about herself now, and she liked it that way.

Don't miss any of the books in SWEET VALLEY HIGH
SENIOR YEAR, an exciting series from Bantam Books!

Visit the Official Sweet Valley Web Site on the Internet at:

www.sweetvalley.com

Francine Pascal's SVH senioryear

Me, Me, Me

CREATED BY
FRANCINE PASCAL

BANTAM BOOKS
NEW YORK · TORONTO · LONDON · SYDNEY · AUCKLAND

RL: 6, AGES 012 AND UP

ME, ME, ME

A Bantam Book / September 2001

Sweet Valley High® is a registered trademark of Francine Pascal.
Conceived by Francine Pascal.
Cover photography by Michael Segal.

Copyright © 2001 by Francine Pascal.
Cover copyright © 2001 by 17th Street Productions,
an Alloy Online, Inc. company.

Produced by 17th Street Productions,
an Alloy Online, Inc. company.
151 West 26th Street
New York, NY 10011.

ISBN: 0-553-49382-5

Visit us on the Web! www.randomhouse.com/teens

Published simultaneously in the United States and Canada

Bantam Books is an imprint of Random House Children's Books, a
division of Random House, Inc. BANTAM BOOKS and the rooster
colophon are registered trademarks of Random House, Inc. Bantam Books,
1540 Broadway, New York, New York 10036.

PRINTED IN THE UNITED STATES OF AMERICA

OPM   0 9 8 7 6 5 4 3 2 1

To Honour and Cyr

TIA RAMIREZ

COULD WINTER BREAK HAVE BEEN ANY SHORTER? I CAN'T BELIEVE IT'S OVER TOMORROW. BUT THEN, I CAN'T BELIEVE A LOT OF THINGS LATELY. LIKE TRENT AND ME. IF SOMEONE HAD TOLD ME A FEW WEEKS AGO I'D BE OVER ANGEL—FOR REAL THIS TIME—AND TOTALLY INTO SOMEONE ELSE BY NOW, I WOULD HAVE LAUGHED. BUT TRENT IS JUST SO INCREDIBLE. WE SAW EACH OTHER ALMOST EVERY DAY OVER BREAK, AND IT FELT SO COMFORTABLE AND EASY. I KNOW IT'S A CLICHÉ, BUT IT'S LIKE WE'VE KNOWN EACH OTHER FOREVER. HOW DID THIS HAPPEN TO ME?

NO, I'M NOT EVEN GOING TO QUESTION IT. I'M JUST GOING TO HANG ON TIGHT WITH BOTH HANDS. DISNEYLAND'S GOT NOTHING ON THIS RIDE.

Ken Matthews

Could winter break have been any longer? This wasn't really the point in my life when I needed extra "at-home" time to hole up in my room and think. At least Dad and I managed to mostly avoid each other. With him working in the day and me seeing Maria at night, we were able to dodge any real conversations about this football scholarship. Which is good because I have no idea what I would say to him. I still can't believe he actually bribed someone to get me into Michigan. I can't believe I'm still considering going. And I can't think anymore about this tonight or I'll go nuts.

I never thought I'd say this, but I can't wait to get back to school.

Evan Plummer

Viva Las Vegas!

All of us—Conner, Jeremy, and I—had the time of our lives. It was totally crazy. Good crazy, not fraught with drama crazy, like so much of my life has been lately. And it's all because I listened to that little voice in my head telling me to take that exit. I didn't think about it. I just went. And you know what? It wasn't that hard.

Maybe that's how life is supposed to be. When you trust that things will work out, they do. It's when you analyze them to death that things turn into a big mess.

So now the voice is at it again. And I'm going to listen to it. It's important to get what you want in this life.

And what I want is Jade.

Elizabeth Wakefield

You know, I've always had priorities. There was school, then there was my family, then Conner, then school again. But lately I've been thinking about that list, and I realized that somebody wasn't on it.

Me.

So I'm readjusting my priorities, and I'm putting myself at number one.

Too impossible? Too unlike the Elizabeth Wakefield we all know and love? Too bad.

Conner and I are over for good, and I've done all the crying and whining about it I can stand. It's time to step outside and do something for myself for a change. And then I'll see the big picture at last.

CHAPTER 1
Obligatory Greetings

Somehow it seemed too early in the morning for the halls at school to be so crazed. Will Simmons had only just walked through the thick glass doors that led to the main lobby, and the echoing voices and crush of students streaming past him were already making his head spin. *Mondays are bad enough,* he thought, *but the Monday just after winter break is cruel and unusual. Can't they find a way to ease us back into school?*

"Simmons!" someone at his left shouted. It was Brian Cogley, from the football team. Will didn't really feel like chatting, so he gave the guy a wave and kept on walking.

When he finally reached his locker, Will stood staring at his lock for a full minute before he could remember the combination. God, had he really been gone that long?

Will sighed and spun the lock. For some reason, the noise in the hallway was really getting to him.

1

Over break he'd spent most of his time at the *Tribune* office, working with Mr. Matthews on the upcoming sporting-events calendar. And he'd hung out with his friends Josh and Matt whenever he had a couple of hours to kill. *I guess I've just gotten used to peace and quiet.* Will shook his head. *Scary.*

The person he hadn't spent much time with was Melissa Fox. Will wondered if she'd noticed. The truth was, he just didn't feel like being around her ever since she'd told Ken Matthews that his father had rigged his football scholarship. Just thinking about it made Will's stomach tie up in knots. He still couldn't believe she'd done that after she *promised* to keep it a secret. Then again, maybe he'd been an idiot to trust her with information like that—he sure regretted it now.

Will's eye fell on the picture of Melissa he had taped to the back of his locker, and he felt a sudden pang. Actually, he'd missed her a lot over break. Even though he was still kind of mad at her, part of him couldn't wait to see her today. Maybe it was time to put this Ken thing in the past. After all, Melissa *had* apologized for blurting out the secret. And he couldn't go on being mad at her forever, could he? Will quickly grabbed the books for his first two classes and slammed the locker shut. Turning, he saw Melissa a few yards away, leaning up against a wall as she chatted with Matt Wells and Josh Radinsky. Will couldn't help himself—he smiled. Melissa was wearing one of his favorite outfits—a short, green skirt and a fuzzy cropped cardigan. She tossed her thick, shiny brown hair back from her shoulders, then gestured wildly with one hand as she held her books tightly with the other. Will chuckled to himself. *She looks so cute when she gets worked up like that,* he thought. *I wonder what she's telling those guys?* He hurried over to join them.

Melissa leaned forward to make her point. She was so intent on what she was saying that she still hadn't noticed Will by the time he was a few feet away from her. Will could hear everything she was saying, and her words stopped him in his tracks.

"—because everybody knows Ken's just not a good enough player for a scholarship like that." Melissa's blue eyes glittered as she spoke, and Matt and Josh seemed to be hanging on her every word. "I mean, *spare me.* Am I supposed to believe that the University of *Michigan* wants SVH's second-string quarterback? If you ask me—"

Will didn't give her time to finish. He grabbed her arm tightly and grinned at his friends. "Hey, guys," he said. He felt Melissa stiffen, but he didn't let go of her arm. "Walk me to class, Melissa?"

Her face was tight, but she said, "Sure."

"Later." Will gave his confused friends a wave as he steered Melissa across the hall and into an alcove by the water fountain. "What do you think you're doing?" he growled.

She gave him a wry little smile. "Hi, Will. It's nice to see you too."

"Cut it out, Liss," he hissed. "I heard you."

"What are you talking about?" Her blue eyes widened in her best impersonation of an innocent person. God, she could be so infuriating. Will forced himself to count to ten.

"You promised me you wouldn't say anything about Ken's scholarship, Melissa," Will said slowly, once he had regained his composure. "We've been at school for, what, ten minutes? Is there anyone you haven't told?"

"I didn't say anything," she said, pouting. "You never let me explain—"

"I *heard* you," Will repeated.

Melissa carefully tugged at both straps of her backpack, looking everywhere but at him. "All I said was that I thought the scholarship seemed weird to me."

"Why did you say *anything*?" Impatient, Will raked his hand through his hair. "What do you want to get those guys all spun up about it for? They'll go tell everybody, and then a whole big rumor will—"

Will stopped himself, then stared at Melissa dead-on. "Wait a minute," he said, his voice dropping. "That's it, isn't it? You figured out a way to get around your promise to me. You won't actually tell anyone

4

what you know. You'll just get suspicions going and then let people figure it out for themselves."

"God, Will." Melissa rolled her eyes. "Don't be so dramatic."

He laughed softly and shook his head. "You know, that's really clever," he said. "Much better than just blurting it out to Ken the way you did."

Melissa lifted her chin, her eyes flashing defiantly. "I didn't know it was such a huge deal to you."

"You *didn't?*" he cried. "Was my not speaking to you for nearly our entire break not enough of a hint?"

"Oh, is that why I didn't see you?" she shot back. "I thought you were just too busy kissing Ken's dad's butt to call me."

One . . . two . . . I am counting very calmly . . . I am very calm right now . . . three, Will told himself. "I'm just going to pretend I didn't hear that," he said. "Here's the deal. Keep your mouth shut from now on, or I swear, Melissa, I'm finished with you. Get it? Not a word."

He didn't wait for an answer. Will just spun away from her and stormed down the hallway. He was furious, and he was sure Melissa felt the same way. He could feel her behind him, still standing there, glaring at him.

Those cool eyes of hers could somehow burn a hole right through you.

*   *   *

5

I should just go to Michigan, Ken thought as he grabbed his history book from the top shelf of his locker. *Who would ever know how I got the stupid scholarship anyway?*

He slammed his locker shut, then watched his beat-up tennis shoes smack against the floor as he headed to third period. *Well, I'd know how I got it.*

As if I could ever forget it.

Ken clenched his jaw and kept his head down as he trudged down the hall. It had been this way ever since he'd found out his dad had rigged his football scholarship. One minute Ken would decide to just go ahead and take it anyway. After all, it was the best deal he had going, now or probably ever. But the next minute he'd want nothing to do with it.

Ken had never been this indecisive in his life. Not even over Maria, and that had been a pretty crazy time.

What if I took it, and then everyone here found out? Of course, by that time I'd be at Michigan anyway, so who cares? But what if everyone at Michigan found out? Including the "real" football players? That could definitely happen. Besides, what about the people who really need that scholarship . . . and really deserve it? It's like I'm stealing money from them—or worse. On the other hand, other places aren't exactly banging down my door, and Michigan means a great football program, not to mention a

6

*first-class education. I could do anything with that
diploma—*

Absentmindedly Ken turned down the hall without looking up. "Whoa!" he heard someone shout. Reflexively he pulled up short just in time to keep from running headlong into Will.

"Sorry." Ken tried to sidestep Will, but in the next instant both of them were pushed up against the wall as a crowd of students flooded out of the gym.

"Like cattle," Will said, and offered Ken a weak smile.

Does he mean them or us? Ken wondered, but he didn't bother asking. He knew Will was just trying to act normal. Ken actually appreciated the effort. He hadn't seen Will since the day Melissa had spilled the truth about his dad. *What can I possibly say to the guy?* Ken thought. *You're cool, but your girlfriend's a nightmare? Dump her before she steals your everlasting soul?* Still, figuring an obligatory greeting was in order, he coughed and asked, "How's it going?"

Will looked at the ceiling. "Actually, it's been better."

"Sounds familiar," Ken agreed. The two of them stared out over the crowd, pretending to be interested in the faces going by. The mad rush went on and on. *We're going to have to make conversation for at least another thirty seconds,* Ken realized with horror.

Will had obviously come to the same conclusion. "Have a good break?" he asked after a moment.

7

Ken shrugged, not wanting to admit it hadn't been much of a break for him at all, between sneaking around to avoid his dad and losing sleep over the scholarship decision. "It was okay," he lied.

Finally the crowd began to thin out, and Will stepped forward. "Well," he said, "take it easy."

Ken watched him turn to leave, suddenly feeling stupid about the way he was acting. "Will—wait a second."

Will turned back to him, eyebrows raised. He looked almost fearful, as if he thought Ken might scream at him or something. Ken nearly laughed. After all, Will was practically the only person who'd been decent about this whole situation . . . not counting Maria, of course.

Ken dug his hands into his pockets. "Look, I just wanted to say . . ." He shrugged. What *did* he want to say? "Thanks, I guess."

Will stood there a moment, then shook his head. "What?" he asked, as if maybe he thought Ken had been speaking French.

Will's expression was so funny that Ken actually laughed. "Listen, I know you didn't want Melissa to tell me about my dad, which I appreciate. Besides, in a way I'm kind of glad she did. At least it's opened my eyes. So, well . . . thanks."

Will thought about that for a moment, then frowned. "You know," he said, "Melissa never would have told you if she thought you'd get an ounce of happiness out of it."

Ken shrugged again. "Well . . . it serves her right, I guess."

Will smiled at that, then nodded quickly. "So anyway," he said, "no need to thank me is what I'm saying. I didn't do anything. And I'm the one who should thank you for not telling your dad that I found out about it. I like it down at the paper. I don't want to screw that up."

"Yeah," Ken said. "It's tough to have something you really want just fall apart on you."

"Tell me about it," Will said sharply.

Ken winced. For a moment he'd forgotten that Will was supposed to get the Michigan scholarship first . . . and for real, without a bribe. Then he'd gotten injured and Ken had taken his place. "I—I didn't mean—"

"Look," Will cut him off, "if you're even considering giving up that scholarship, you'd better think again. You know how many guys would do *anything* for a chance like that?"

Ken stared at him. Will's eyes were a hard blue that locked onto his own.

"And I mean *anything*," Will said. He clapped Ken firmly on the shoulder. "Just don't do something you'll regret later, okay? I've gotta run."

Ken watched Will walk away, then he turned and

headed down the hallway and into history class, slipping quietly into his chair. What Will had said made a lot of sense. He should be grateful for this chance, no matter how it had come his way.

Shouldn't I?

Ken pressed his hands against his eyes, feeling as confused as ever.

Evan was on the wrong floor and about a mile away from his next class. But he had a few minutes left before the bell. And he wanted to see if Jade was around. Ever since he'd gotten back from Arizona, she'd been the last thing on his mind when he'd clicked off his lamp every night and his first thought when he opened his eyes. Was he falling for her again? Or had he never really gotten over her in the first place? Maybe just seeing her would jolt him out of it.

Then again, maybe not.

There she was, leaning against a row of lockers and talking to Cherie Reese. She looked fantastic in a pair of low-slung jeans and a tight red sweater. But Jade always looked great, no matter what she was wearing.

He took a step toward her, then hesitated. *Why* had they broken up again? For a second he really couldn't remember. And then it hit him like a punch in the gut—Elizabeth. Jade had been jealous of her, and it had nearly cost him his friendship with Conner. Evan smiled wryly to himself. There was a time when he'd been head over heels for Elizabeth. It had felt like such a huge deal at the time, but the whole memory was fuzzy now, all blurred at the edges. He could remember that he'd had feelings for Elizabeth, but he couldn't call them up anymore. They were long gone. But his feelings for Jade were still crystal clear.

Jade threw her hair back over her shoulder and laughed at something Cherie said. Evan remembered that laugh. The sound of it sent shock waves through his body, and for a moment he was completely transfixed.

What will happen if we get back together? We tried it once; maybe it just isn't meant to be—

Wait a minute, he commanded himself. *Stop right there, brain.* Hadn't he resolved to stop analyzing everything to death? To quit worrying over the details and just go with his instincts? Hadn't Vegas taught him anything?

So just walk over there and talk to her.

Evan shoved his hands into his pockets and shuffled across the hallway. Cherie saw him first, and she muttered a quick, "See ya," to Jade before walking away. Jade watched her go. An expression of confusion crossed her face, and then she looked up and saw Evan.

"Hey," he said to her.

"Oh." Her eyes went big, and she took a step backward. "Um, hi."

11

Evan took a deep breath, then blew it out. He looked down the hallway, then turned and looked toward the other end, trying to avoid her eyes. Something about them bothered him. Like they wanted to know what he was doing here. And he wasn't sure he was ready to answer that question. "So how have you been?" he asked. He ran a hand through his hair, brushing a few strands back from his eyes. "Did you have a good—"

Just then the bell rang, jangling through the halls like an alarm. Jade looked behind her, through the classroom door, then back at Evan. She gave him a tiny smile and shrugged.

Evan smiled back, feeling like an idiot. "Guess you'd better get going," he said. Then, just as she was turning away, he added, "Catch you later?"

Jade hesitated a moment, then nodded. "Yeah," she said, "okay," and ducked inside her class.

Evan turned and sprinted down the stairway and then across the first-floor hall. *Well, I have no idea how that went,* he realized. *She didn't exactly seem thrilled to see me. Then again, what did I expect? A marching band and a laser light show?* At least they'd made contact. And she'd even smiled—kind of. Evan grinned as he slid into his seat.

Funny how that little half smile from Jade had just lit up his whole day.

Melissa Fox

Will's problem is that he just doesn't understand that I only have his best interests at heart. Why should he go around protecting Ken? I mean, has Will already forgotten that Ken practically stole everything from him? Like his spot on the football team? And the Michigan scholarship? And—at one point—even _me_?

Ken can't be trusted. Believe me, I know. I had to learn the hard way-getting dumped for Maria-but I learned, all right. Ken deserves everything that's coming to him.

Why doesn't Will get that I'm only doing this for him?

Ken Matthews

I've always heard when you can't make a decision, you should write down all the reasons for and against it. Well, I can't concentrate on history anyway, so here goes.

Why I should take the scholarship:

-It's a great opportunity, and opportunities don't come along every day.

-It doesn't mean I don't deserve it. They wouldn't take me if I was a total loser, no matter who my father is.

-If I don't take it, my father will go ballistic.

Why I shouldn't take it:

-I didn't earn it.

-I don't like taking a free ride on one of my dad's deals.

-If I don't take it, my father will go ballistic.

CHAPTER
Like Fate or Something
2

A pack of gray squirrels chased each other around a tree outside, chattering loudly enough to be heard even through the closed window of the *Oracle* office. Elizabeth gazed at them, her chin in her hand. *At least somebody's showing some spirit today,* she thought glumly.

Her first day back at school, and already she was bored and restless, only half listening to Mr. Collins make announcements for the upcoming semester. Pretty pathetic, actually, when just last night she'd had so much energy and determination. Last semester had been such a waste, she'd resolved to make a fresh start today. She had to make herself top priority for a change.

This morning she'd resolved to do things differently. But now here it was not even lunch, and she was already back in her old routine. All morning she'd had to face the usual greetings from friends, all of them wanting to know how her break had gone.

15

"Just great," she'd said, managing to smile at every one of them. After all, what was she *supposed* to say? That she'd spent most of her time at the Wakefield family reunion replaying the whole breakup with Conner—wondering over and over again just why and how it had happened—and the rest of her time taking long walks through the neighborhood and even longer soaks in the tub?

Now she watched as two of the squirrels broke away from the others. They sprinted across a sidewalk, then up the trunk of a red maple, disappearing into the leafy branches at the top.

Even those squirrels are in a good relationship, she thought miserably, then caught herself. *I can't let a couple of rodents make me feel bad about myself,* Elizabeth decided. *This is the new, self-confident, independent Elizabeth.* She forced herself to concentrate on Mr. Collins.

". . . and this particular program will only be made available to seniors this semester," he was saying. "As most of you know, the *Scope* is the region's oldest newsmagazine, with a long history of concise reporting, and this internship will mean—"

Wait a minute, did he say the Scope? Elizabeth looked at the address and phone number that Mr. Collins had written on the board. Sure enough, *Scope* was written at the top, and Mr. Collins was droning on and on about some of the major journalism awards the magazine had won over the years. He didn't need to sell Elizabeth on how great that magazine was. Her father had subscribed to it for years, and she was always picking up stray copies around the house and reading whatever caught her eye. Their news stories were top rated, and their local features were always interesting and well written. Was he actually saying she might have a chance to work there?

". . . allowing you to receive professional publication experience while you earn class credit as well," Mr. Collins concluded.

Class credit *too?* Okay, this was too much. It had to be fate or something—just the opportunity she'd been looking for. This could be her chance to branch out of creative writing and get back into the types of stories she knew something about. She could learn to write real, hard news pieces—not like her articles for the *Oracle,* but stories she would really have to throw herself into, that the whole town could read and learn something from.

Not to mention, of course, that it would help take her mind off Conner.

Elizabeth looked around to see how her classmates were responding to this announcement, wondering what kind of competition she might be facing. She expected to see everyone looking as eager as she felt. But only a few of them even seemed to be listening. It was a busy time of year, after all, with college applications and campus visits and all the senior and graduation events coming up. Most people probably couldn't spare the time. In fact, Elizabeth was pretty much booked herself these days, with her class load and her job at Sedona. But she was sure she could handle it. Especially now that she wasn't seeing anyone. *Hey, being pathetically dateless has its perks*, she told herself.

Jen Graft, though, seemed to be listening intently to the *Scope* information. She sat with her hand raised, leaning forward in her chair, until Mr. Collins called on her.

"Yes, Jen?" he said.

"How much does it pay?" Jen asked eagerly.

"It's an unpaid internship," Mr. Collins said. "You earn experience and class credit. No money, I'm afraid."

That seemed to do it for Jen. She frowned and began doodling in her notebook.

Elizabeth flung open her own notebook and quickly jotted down the *Scope*'s number from the board, feeling her earlier energy practically surging back now. Maybe this would be her fresh start after all. Her chance to make a huge splash in the big-time world of real journalism, to write a piece that would wake people up, change the world, win her the Pulitzer . . .

Or not. Anyway, it beat squirrel watching.

Just before lunch Evan saw Jade again, this time at her locker. He watched as she slid her books onto the top shelf, then looked into the little mirror hanging on her locker door. She pulled out a brush and ran it through her black hair. Just watching her do that sent a small jolt of electricity through his body. He loved her hair—loved the way it swung just at her shoulders and could turn almost blue under the lights.

Try again, said the little voice in his head, so he walked up behind her and tapped her on the shoulder. Jade wheeled around and flashed him a broad smile. But then she seemed to remember something, and just as quickly as it came, the smile was gone.

"Oh. Hi, Evan," she said.

"Hi." Evan leaned against the locker next to hers. "So—how's it going?"

Jade gave him a sort of smile and cocked her head. "Pretty good."

"Good." *She's wondering what I'm doing here,* he realized, and the thought made Evan so self-conscious that suddenly he couldn't think of a single thing to say. "That's good." *What next?* he wondered. "So, how was your break?" he finally asked. *Lame. God, how lame.*

"Good," she replied, but the look on her face told him that she was waiting for him to say something else. But what?

You know what, the voice in his head answered.

"Yeah, I'm glad they give us that break between semesters," Evan said in a rush. He stopped to clear his throat. He was into it now. He might as well play it out. "It's always good when you get to start with a clean slate." He stepped toward her and looked into her dark eyes. "Especially," he said softly, "if you got a lot of things wrong the last time around."

Jade's eyebrows flew up, and for a moment she stood perfectly still. She seemed to think about that for a moment, then shrugged. "Interesting observation," she said slowly, almost carefully. "So how was *your* break?"

Evan wasn't really sure whether Jade understood that he'd been trying to apologize, but somehow he felt that he didn't want to clarify by coming out and saying that he was sorry he'd ended things. After all, he really had no idea how Jade felt. And Evan knew that Jade could be kind of explosive—better to ease into things now and get into the heavy stuff later. "My break was pretty good," he said. "Do anything fun?"

"I saw about five hundred movies," she said. "I thought I'd go blind."

Okay, now ask her which movies she saw, Evan

thought, but he just couldn't bring himself to do it. All of this chitchat was driving him crazy, when what he really wanted to be doing was asking Jade out. "You want to have coffee sometime?" he heard himself blurt.

"I—I—" Jade's eyes went wide, and after a moment she started to laugh. "Okay," she said, shrugging, "why not?"

Evan wasn't sure why Jade was cracking up. He suspected that she might be laughing at him and felt his face turn hot. *Then again,* he told himself, *I asked her out and she said yes, and that's really all that matters.* He decided to forge ahead. "Great. When?"

Jade thought about it. "I'm pretty busy today and tomorrow," she said. "But I could meet you on Wednesday. After basketball practice."

"Wednesday's great." Evan felt his blush disappear. Now he could just feel himself grinning like a fool.

Jade scanned the hallway. "I think we'd better get going." Evan followed her gaze. Only a couple of students were left now, hanging out near their classroom doors. "So I'll see you at HOJ on Wednesday, then."

"Yeah," Evan said. "See you." He watched her turn and head down the hall, that hair of hers gleaming under the lights. In a daze he walked toward the lunchroom, feeling like he was in some kind of dream or something.

A dream that had just come true.

*   *   *

The second the *Oracle* meeting was over, Elizabeth dashed into the hall to the nearest pay phone. Even though no one else had seemed too psyched over the intern job, she wasn't taking any chances on someone beating her to the punch. She fumbled in her backpack for change, then pushed the coins into the slot. Nervously she dialed the number for the *Scope* and stood tapping her nails against the wall while the phone rang.

"*Sweet Valley Scope*," said a woman's voice. "Dora speaking."

"Uh, hi," Elizabeth said. "I'm a student at Sweet Valley High, and I just heard about an internship program that's available to our class this semester. I was wondering—"

"Right," said Dora, "the work-study program."

"Yes, that's the one," Elizabeth agreed, trying to sound overly friendly but not overly eager. It was a tough mix. "Is the job still open?"

"Oh, absolutely." Dora's voice sounded bored.

Elizabeth hesitated, then asked, "Would you be able to tell me a little about it?" A couple of freshmen walked by, singing at the top of their lungs. Elizabeth stuck a finger in one ear to try to drown out the noise from the hallway.

"Well, you'll actually need to speak with Ms. Perry," Dora explained. "She's the managing editor, and she'll be doing the hiring for the position. But from what I understand, they need help with everything—filing, typing. . . . I even need some help with these phones here."

Typing and answering phones? "Oh." Elizabeth tried to keep the disappointment out of her voice. "Well, do they need writers too?"

"I don't really know, but it's possible, seeing as they're looking for someone with good writing skills. We've had several applicants, but none has been a good fit so far, if you want to know the truth." Elizabeth could hear Dora typing as she continued the conversation. "Do you have journalism experience?"

"Oh, definitely," Elizabeth said. She'd been ready for that one. "I'm the editor of our school newspaper, and I've written tons of features and editorials for it." Elizabeth dug in her pocket for the small scrap of paper where she'd made notes on her related experience. "And I work on my own writing all the time—short stories and poems and things. But I'm mostly interested in writing real news—you know, local reporting on current issues and events." Glancing at the paper, she added, "Oh, I take AP English, and I have an A in that class. I also take a creative-writing course. . . ."

"What did you say your name was again?" Dora had stopped typing. "You definitely sound qualified, and we're kind of swamped. We need someone down here ASAP."

Elizabeth broke into a grin. "My name is Elizabeth Wakefield," she said. "*W-a-k- e*—"

"Can you get down here right away?"

Elizabeth sucked in a breath, hoping Dora hadn't heard. "Sure!" she said. "When would you like—"

"Can you make it this afternoon? Ms. Perry will be here around three-thirty. I'm sure she'll want to talk to you."

"Oh," Elizabeth said, her heart sinking. She had to work at Sedona this afternoon! "Could we make it tomorrow instead?"

"I'm sorry," said Dora, "but they're coming up on deadline soon, and things get pretty hectic. If you can't make it today, Ms. Perry won't be able to see you until next week."

Elizabeth twirled a piece of hair around her finger while she weighed her options. A week seemed too long to wait. Besides, this job was way more important than handing out lipstick samples.

Hey, you're top priority now, she reminded herself. *Go for it.*

"Okay," she said. "This afternoon will be fine." Elizabeth quickly dug a pen out of her purse and flipped over the piece of scrap paper she'd been reading from so she could jot down directions to the

office. She said good-bye to Dora, then hung up the phone only to pick it right back up again. She punched in the number for Sedona.

"Sedona, for a beautiful you," said the voice on the other end. "How can I help you?" It was Carolee.

"Hi, it's Elizabeth." She'd made her voice as thick and slow as possible and now threw in a sniffle and two small coughs. "I've got this terrible headache," she said. "And I think I'm catching a cold or something." Elizabeth waved happily at Andy Marsden as he passed by, then caught herself and felt a pang of guilt. *Oh, get over it,* she told herself firmly. *You hardly ever call in sick, and someone can cover your shift for one day.* "I'm sorry, but I just don't think I'll be able to come in today."

"You sound terrible!" Carolee's voice was concerned. "You get some rest and make sure to drink lots of juice."

Elizabeth smiled at the receiver. "I will," she promised.

"Don't push yourself," Carolee warned. "Don't worry about us here. It's more important for you to get well."

"Thanks—I'm sure I'll be better tomorrow. See you." Elizabeth hung up the phone. Yes, she was sure she would be better tomorrow. If she got the job, that is.

* * *

Jessica Wakefield scanned the lunchroom as she filed out behind Tia Ramirez. No sign of her sister. "Where is Elizabeth?" Jessica demanded. "She never misses lunch. Do you think she went home sick or something?"

Tia rolled her eyes. "And I thought Liz was the mother hen. You're just as bad, Jess. Maybe worse."

"I know, but it's *cute* when I do it." Jessica glanced around again, but no luck. "Besides, you should have seen her at our family reunion. All she did was sit around, moping over Conner." Jessica didn't want to say so, but she was actually a little worried about Elizabeth. When her twin got into those moping moods, it could be hard to snap her out of them.

"Maybe she just got caught up with something," Tia suggested.

I'll bet, Jessica thought. *Caught up writing depressing poetry about love and betrayal.* Suddenly she stopped in her tracks. "I'm going to check the library," she said.

Tia nodded. "That's so crazy, it just might work."

"Later." Jessica gave Tia a quick wave and hurried down the hall. Naturally, nobody would ever expect to catch Jessica in the library on the first day back from winter break. But she was almost certain that she would find her sister there.

Sure enough, Elizabeth was at her favorite

table—the third on the left—furiously scribbling notes from one of a dozen books lying open in front of her. Jessica walked up behind her and scanned the titles. *Magazine Article Writing, Editing for Paper and Print,* and a bunch of other boring stuff.

Jessica flopped into the chair across from her sister. "You should really try a romance novel once in a while," she said, giving her silky blond hair a toss. "Definitely more exciting."

Elizabeth didn't even look up from her mad scribbling. "Who needs romance when your dream job awaits you?" she asked in a low voice.

"Dream job?" Jessica cried.

"Jess, keep it down," Elizabeth whispered, "we're in a library."

Jessica looked around. They were the only two people there. Even the librarian seemed to have disappeared. But Jessica knew better than to argue with her sister. She lowered her voice and asked, "What dream job?"

"An internship at the *Sweet Valley Scope,*" Elizabeth said. She grinned, then added, "I've got an interview there later today, and I want to sound like I know what I'm talking about."

"The *Scope*?" Jessica asked. "You mean that boring newsmagazine Dad's always reading?"

Elizabeth frowned. "Jessica, it's a very serious

magazine—they've won a ton of awards."

Elizabeth looked hurt, and Jessica felt a twinge of guilt. "Sorry, Liz. I'm sure it's great. It sounds perfect for you."

"I know," Elizabeth said, her face flushed with color. "It's like fate or something. And you know what the best part is?"

"You get a free subscription?"

Elizabeth rolled her eyes. "The best part is I'll be getting real magazine experience. It could actually help me decide on a career down the road."

Jessica nodded, resisting the urge to roll *her* eyes. It seemed like every time Elizabeth got a little excited over something, it became all tied up in her entire life's goals. But she *was* truly happy for her sister. Although . . . Jessica glanced around at the crowd of books on the table in front of Elizabeth. Her sister could get a little—intense about things sometimes. Like with Conner. Part of Jessica had to wonder if this newspaper thing was just a way for Elizabeth to channel her feelings about her ex into a new hobby. *But is that necessarily a bad thing?* Jessica wondered. *Aren't you supposed to distract yourself after a breakup?*

". . . and I was just thinking how last semester was such a total waste, you know? I really need to dive into something new."

Jessica nodded. Maybe her sister was right—she really did need something totally new to think about. "It's great, Liz," she said. "I'm really proud of you. Just try to take it easy, okay? You know how you get."

Elizabeth blinked at her. "How can I get?" Her eyes strayed from Jessica to the book laid out before her. Clearly she was ready to get back to her reading. *Oh, well,* Jessica decided. *Let her. I'll just find a way to make sure that she gets out once in a while. Otherwise she'll end up burying herself under these books for the next twenty years.*

"Never mind," Jessica said. "Good luck with the interview."

She left Elizabeth sitting in the library, staring after her, and headed toward class. Jessica shook her head as she walked down the hall, wondering if there wasn't some kind of twelve-step program for extremely intense sisters.

Jade Wu

Top-five possible reasons
Evan asked me to coffee:

5. He likes me again.
4. He's missed talking to me.
3. He needs caffeine.
2. It wasn't Evan—it was his evil twin!
1. <u>He likes me again?</u>

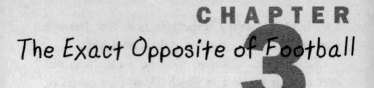
"I know it's fast," Tia was saying to Jessica as they changed out of their sweats after cheerleading practice. They were huddled in a corner of the girls' locker room, oblivious to the other members of the squad, who were caught up in their own conversations. "Believe me, I know more than anybody how fast it seems. But it's definitely right, you know? It *feels* right."

Jessica nodded, grinning at how Tia kept going on and on about Trent. She'd spent practically the entire lunch period listening to the stories of how Tia and Trent had spent their whole break together, taking long drives in the afternoons and having picnics on the beach, and now Tia was at it again full force. Not that Jessica minded. It was nice to see her friend so swept off her feet—and so obviously over Angel.

Jessica took a pair of clean socks from her gym bag and began to put them on. "You don't have to sell me on the idea, Tee," she said. "I'm just so glad you

31

and Trent are dating. Especially now that Jeremy's staying with him for the rest of the school year."

Tia grinned. "I know. You and I can hang out over at their house and watch TV or play games or something."

"We can see movies together . . . ," Jessica said.

"And rent videos together . . ."

"And drive to the beach together . . ."

The two girls looked at each other, then started to laugh.

Just then Coach Laufeld entered the locker room. She had her clipboard in front of her and was tapping her pen against it as she looked around the room. "Okay," she called out, "listen up, girls." The room fell silent as everyone on the cheer squad turned to face the coach. "I've got a couple of announcements, both due to Cherie and Jade's decision to quit the squad and join the basketball team. Since we need to fill their spots, we're going to have open auditions on Wednesday afternoon and a special evening pep rally after that to demonstrate our best cheers to the new girls trying out."

"Oh, cool," Jessica said breathlessly. This was the perfect opportunity to drag Elizabeth out among the living. *She's got to learn to balance the social with the . . . mental, or whatever,* Jessica decided. *All work and no play makes Elizabeth a dull twin.*

32

"I want to do a full run-through before the tryouts, so everyone needs to be here for practice at four-thirty. Got it? Don't be late." With that, the coach left the room, and the buzz of voices started in again.

"An evening pep rally sounds cool," Tia said. "Think the guys will come?"

The *guys*. Jessica just loved the sound of that. Like they were this set, tight group. "Well, we'll have to make sure they leave their Big Mesa jackets at home that day," she said, giggling. "But I'm sure they'll come."

And she knew it was true. Everyone who was important to her would be there, if she had anything to say about it.

Including her favorite twin.

Ken came home after school and flung open the door of his house. "Hello?" he called, then breathed a sigh of relief when there was no answer. *Good,* he thought, *Dad isn't home yet.* He could really use some time alone to veg. Not that he hadn't been a complete walking stalk of broccoli all day at school. It was such a joke. He couldn't concentrate in class, couldn't focus on his friends—he couldn't even give poor Maria a break. He knew he'd been leaning on her hard, whining to her about this whole scholarship thing until she was probably about to become as manic as he was. If he kept up like this, he was going to flunk his senior year, and then he wouldn't have to worry about college at all.

Maybe that's not such a bad idea, Ken thought wryly as he shuffled into the kitchen. He stood staring into the refrigerator for the longest time. Nothing looked the least bit appealing to him. Finally he grabbed a can of Coke, then headed back to the living room. On his way out he spotted a bag of Doritos.

He snatched the bag and went into the living room, then flopped down on the couch, ready to munch and chill out in front of the tube for a few minutes and let his brain rest. No more should he or shouldn't he. Just for five minutes.

But the second he flipped on the TV, the phone rang. It figured. Probably his dad calling to tell him he'd be late. Ken hoped so. He'd love to have the place all to himself tonight. Ken pressed the mute button and reached for the receiver.

"Hello?"

"Ken! It's Hank Krubowski."

Immediately Ken felt a hard knot tighten in his stomach. "Oh," he mumbled. "Hi." He briefly considered saying a sarcastic congratulations on Krubowski's new assistant-coaching position—the bribe Ken's dad arranged in exchange for the scholarship—but somehow he couldn't even joke about it.

"I was calling to see if you and your dad are free on Wednesday evening," Krubowski said. "Coach Garrett and I would like to take you both out for dinner. You know, just to chat and answer any questions you might have about Michigan. And of course, to go over the details of your scholarship. We'll have a letter of intent for you to take home and sign."

Ken struggled to focus, thinking wildly of what he should say. Obviously he should say no. The very idea of sitting through an entire meal with his dad and Krubowski made him want to hurl. Then again . . .

"Ken?" Krubowski said. "You still there?"

Ken swallowed hard and took a deep breath. Quickly his mind searched for something appropriate to say. "Did you say Coach Garrett was coming too?"

"Yeah, he'll be there," Krubowski said. "A really nice guy. You'll love working with him, Ken."

"Huh," Ken muttered. The fact was, there was really no reason to assume that Coach Garrett knew anything about the bribe. After all, the word on the street was that the Michigan coach was old school—tough but fair. Supposedly he took good care of his players. Ken had wanted to meet him for a while.

"So we're on for Wednesday, then," Krubowski said.

"Well," Ken said, "I'll have to check with my dad."

"I'll go ahead and make the reservations. If your father can't make it, you call me back tonight, okay?"

Man, could this guy be pushier? "Um, yeah, sure," Ken said. He guessed it would be okay just to talk with these guys. At least it would buy him more time to decide.

He hung up the phone, thinking for a second that he should probably call his dad and make sure it was okay. But then he decided not to bother. His father would cancel open-heart surgery if it meant meeting the Michigan coach.

Immediately the same old arguments started up in his head. *I just can't go. I don't deserve it. It's not fair to me or anybody else. But how can I give up something so great? I may never get this kind of chance again. And who cares how I got it? Everyone gets some help with these things, don't they? It's all about who you know. . . .*

He stared at the television, realizing he had no idea what he was watching anymore or what was going on. Even the Doritos didn't do it for him now.

So much for taking his mind off Michigan. He picked up the phone and dialed Maria. Soft, warm, sexy Maria. The exact opposite of football. He had to talk to her for a minute just to clear his head.

Luckily the inside of the elevator doors was a shiny chrome, and Elizabeth was able to inspect herself from head to toe as she rode up the five floors to the *Scope* office. She'd changed clothes so quickly after school, she hadn't really had a chance to survey the results. Yes, her navy suit was clean and not too wrinkled, the white blouse beneath crisp and professional looking. Even her hair, hastily pinned up off her shoulders, looked acceptable. She slicked on a little more lip gloss and pressed her lips together. This interview *had* to go well. If she didn't get this internship, she'd be devastated. *Think positively,* she told herself, just as the doors opened.

She stepped out into a lobby with clean white walls and a gray marble counter sitting squarely in the center. The floors were carpeted in deep blue, and down the first hallway she could see light gray partitions. *The newsroom,* she thought, excitement building in her chest. If she listened hard enough, she thought she could even hear the light tapping of keyboards. God, she just had to nail this interview!

Elizabeth stepped up to the counter to see a plump woman with short gray hair and glasses staring at a computer monitor. "Hi," she said. "I'm Elizabeth Wakefield. I'm here to speak to Ms. Perry."

The woman looked up at her and squinted. "Oh, yes . . . Elizabeth. I'm Dora. We spoke on the phone." The woman stood up and held out her hand.

"Nice to meet you." Elizabeth shook the woman's hand, concentrating on having a handshake that was firm but not too overbearing.

"You'll be interviewing in here." Dora led her

down the hallway and opened the first door on the right. Inside was an open, spacious room with a huge table in the center and at least a dozen chairs around it. "Have a seat," she said. "I'll tell her you're here."

Elizabeth sat down and opened the bag she had brought with her. It was just big enough to hold a manila folder, a steno book, and two pens. She took out the folder and spread her résumé, references, and *Oracle* clippings on the table just as a slim, pretty woman in a black pantsuit opened the door.

"Hi, Elizabeth." The woman slid into the seat across from her. "I'm Joanna Perry. Thanks for coming down here on such short notice."

Elizabeth smiled. "Oh, I'm happy to do it, Ms. Perry."

The woman waved her hand dismissively. "Call me Joanna. Or Jo, if you like. Can I see what you've got there?" She pointed to Elizabeth's résumé.

Elizabeth handed it to her, then sat uncomfortably while Joanna looked it over. She bit at her nail, then forced herself to stop. *Silence can't be good,* she thought. *Think of something to say.*

"The *Scope* is such a great publication," Elizabeth said, instantly kicking herself for the waver in her voice. She cleared her throat. "I've always loved it. My dad's had a subscription for years. He always says it's so professional." *So professional?* Elizabeth struggled not to cringe. *I just made the* Scope *sound like a third-grade newsletter!*

Luckily Joanna didn't seem to take offense. Instead she just laughed and said, "Well, I'm glad it *looks* professional, at least." She ran a hand through her short red hair. "We've been so swamped lately, I feel like we're hanging by our fingernails. One of our advertisers pulled out at the last minute today—a huge, four-color ad—and now we have to fill the space before deadline. Not to mention that we'll be losing revenue." She waved her hand in the air. "But that's typical. It's always something here."

"Oh," Elizabeth said, a little unsure of how to respond. Then she added, "Sounds like you could use some help."

Joanna grinned. "You read my mind. Can I see some of your writing?"

Elizabeth handed Joanna her *Oracle* clips. "As you can see, I've done a lot of interviews and opinion pieces, but I also like the harder investigative stuff." She was just getting ready to mention her creative-writing class when Joanna stopped her.

"Look," she said. "I can tell you now, you're definitely qualified. But I've got to be honest with you. I'm a little worried you might get too bored with this job."

Bored? "Oh, I don't think I could ever get—"

"This is a magazine," Joanna interrupted, "and so

we do need people with strong writing and editing backgrounds. That way if we need to fill in those roles later on, we'll have them already on hand. But I have to tell you that the position we need filled right now is more of a gofer one. We need someone to answer phones and take messages, type correspondence and mail it, stuff envelopes with promotions for subscribers, things like that."

Elizabeth nodded. Even though she'd known that she wouldn't exactly be starting out with her own by-line, she'd hoped that Joanna would at least be able to mention *some* creative aspects to the job. This didn't really sound like the dream job she'd hoped for.

"Does any of that appeal to you?" The woman's green eyes locked on Elizabeth's. "Like I say, there should be an opportunity for more interesting work later on. I just can't promise it now."

Elizabeth bit her bottom lip, trying hard to think quickly. So it wasn't exactly what she'd been hoping for. On the other hand, any job with a real magazine would look good on her résumé and could lead to a better job later. *Everyone pays their dues,* Elizabeth thought. After a moment she shrugged and said, "I'd be happy just to get my foot in the door for now. I can do whatever you need."

Joanna gave her a warm smile. "Well, then," she said, "the internship is yours."

"Really?" Elizabeth said. "Oh, thank you!"

"You'll have to get all the paperwork signed by Mr. Collins and your school principal, of course."

"Of course. No problem." Elizabeth stood up and shook Joanna's hand. It was all she could do to keep from hugging the woman.

"Dora will give you all the paperwork you need," Joanna said. "It was great meeting you. I'll see you the day after tomorrow."

"Yes—day after tomorrow." Elizabeth stood while Joanna left the room, then hastily gathered her clips and made her way to the front desk.

Dora looked up and smiled at her. "I heard," she said before Elizabeth could tell her about getting the job. She picked up a mound of papers and handed them to Elizabeth. "Here's your paperwork—an application form and an employee-policy handbook—and a couple of back issues of the magazine. Congratulations."

"Thanks!" Elizabeth took the stack of papers and cradled them against her chest. "I'll see you soon!" she called over her shoulder as she hurried to the elevator and pushed the button.

Once the shiny doors were closed, Elizabeth once again looked herself over—only this time she grinned. *I got the job!* And no matter what kind of work she started out with, she *would* write something for the *Scope* before the internship was over.

All she had to do was come up with something really juicy—*sexy,* as they said in the publishing world. A sexy little article that would pull in readers and send copies flying off the store shelves.

Well, okay, maybe she was getting a little carried away. Just seeing her name in a byline would be enough for now. All she had to do was come up with something really interesting.

She was sure she could do it. She just needed to focus.

Maria Slater

Why am I so worried about this Michigan thing?

I mean, it's not my scholarship that we're talking about here. And let's face it—I should be more concerned about my scholarship. I've been killing myself just to keep up with my classes. If I let my GPA drop, I can forget the Senate scholarship and all the time and effort it took to get it.

But somehow all I can think about is Ken and his Michigan decision. Which is ridiculous because I'm not even telling him my opinion of the whole thing! (I know it sounds crazy, but I just think he needs to figure it out for himself.)

Anyway, I think it's time to focus on my own problems. Just for a little while, at least.

CHAPTER 4
Too Much Everything

"It won't be for long. Just an hour or so," Jessica promised the next day at lunch. She hoped she didn't sound too whiny—Elizabeth hated it when she whined—but she really wanted her sister to come to the pep rally. Jessica stabbed at her salad with her fork, wishing the school cafeteria wasn't so loud today. It was hard to yell above the noise and *not* sound whiny.

"I just don't know," Elizabeth said. She had one of her library books lying open beside her, and she stared at it as she picked up half of her sandwich. "I've really got a lot going on right now."

From across the table Tia raised her eyebrows and leaned forward. *Try harder,* her look said. As if! Did Tia think that Jessica was going to give up after only twenty minutes of trying to talk Elizabeth into coming? Hardly. Jessica was only getting warmed up.

"Look, Liz," Jessica began, "it's not like you're going to have to totally ditch your shift at the *Scope*

44

or anything. You can just come to the rally right after you get off. Don't they let you go around six o'clock?"

"Supposedly," Elizabeth said. "But I just don't know what things will be like there yet. They might need me to stay all night or something."

"All *night?*" Jessica cried. "On your first day there?" She stared at her sister, who was still trying to read her book. Jessica leaned over and flipped it shut.

Elizabeth sighed and opened the book again, trying to find her page. "Jess, give me a break. I'm kidding about all night." She rolled her eyes. "It's just an expression."

Tia leaned toward Elizabeth, a serious look in her dark eyes. "But do you think they'll really expect you to work so hard? I mean, you have school and another job and everything. Besides, you're just an intern."

Jessica winced, knowing Elizabeth wasn't going to appreciate that last remark. Sure enough, Elizabeth frowned. "Thanks a lot, Tee," she said.

Tia took a swig from her water bottle and set it back down with a thud. "You know what I mean," she protested. "You're an *un*paid employee. As in, not obligated to camp out at your desk until all hours."

Jessica nodded and leaned in closer to her twin. "Right," she said. "You don't owe them all your time and energy when they're not even paying you."

Even as the words left her mouth, she knew she

shouldn't have said them. Elizabeth threw her a dark look and said, "This has nothing to do with money." She wiped her mouth with her napkin and turned her attention back to her book.

Jessica looked at Tia desperately, and then a thought struck her. Elizabeth loved playing big sister more than anything. Why hadn't she remembered that before? "Look," she said slowly, "the thing is, I could really use your support, Liz. This rally is important to me, and it would be great if I could just see your face out there."

Now Elizabeth looked up from her book, her aqua eyes darkening in concern. *Aha! Am I good or am I good?* "Oh," Elizabeth said. "Really? I mean . . . I guess I hadn't thought about it that way. . . ."

Jessica looked over at Tia, who chimed in, "Trent and Jeremy will be at the rally, Liz." She smiled innocently. "And I'd really like you and Trent to become friends. You've hardly spoken three words to him ever. He's starting to believe you're some figment of my imagination."

Elizabeth smiled. "Well," she said, "I can't argue with that." She picked up a carrot stick and bit off the end, chewing thoughtfully.

Jessica could read her sister like nobody else could—she knew that Elizabeth was about to crumble. All she needed was that extra little prod. "It would really mean a lot to both of us, Lizzie," Jessica said.

"Okay, okay," Elizabeth said finally. "But I can only come for a little while." She pointed at Jessica with the carrot stick, emphasizing her words. "And I can't go out after either. I've just got too much—"

"We know, we know." Jessica rolled her eyes, but she was smiling. "Too much everything." She reached out and squeezed her sister's hand. "Thanks, Liz. Believe me, I won't forget this."

And hopefully, neither will you, Jessica thought. A little fun could do a lot for her sister. Jessica knew that better than anybody. And if Elizabeth could just loosen up even a tiny bit, Jessica could stop with the worrying and get back to having more fun herself.

"Ken, you're hardly getting any food here," Maria said, studying his nearly empty lunch tray. She leaned across him and took a sandwich from one of the glassed-off bins along the serving line. "There," she said, setting it on their tray. "You love ham and cheese, right?"

"I don't know if I'm in the mood for it," Ken said. "Well, maybe. Thanks." As usual, he felt anything but hungry.

Maria set her own selections down on the tray—a plate of spaghetti and meatballs and a side of fruit salad—as they moved farther down the serving line.

So here she was, looking out for him as usual. He didn't know what he'd do without her. Probably end up as the first person in the history of the world to starve to death over a college decision.

"How about an apple too?" Maria plunked a shiny Granny Smith down on his tray before he could answer.

Ken grinned at her, then put an arm across her shoulders and gave her a squeeze.

"What?" she asked. Her dark eyes sparkled warmly, but even their glow couldn't hide the note of worry behind them. He knew that he was making her a wreck too. She should be concentrating on classes and committees and all the other things she had going on—not on him and his stupid scholarship.

"Thanks," he said.

Maria lifted her eyebrows. "For what?"

"For taking such good care of me." He took her hand and kissed her fingertips.

Maria leaned against his chest and smiled up at him. Ken held her tighter.

"How am I going to get through that dinner tomorrow without you?" he whispered into her hair.

She leaned back quickly and looked at him in the eye. "You want me to come with you?" she asked sharply.

Ken looked at her a moment, confused. Did she

really think he was serious when he said that? "No. I mean, yes, I want you to—but . . . I was just kidding. . . ."

"Oh," Maria said. Then, "Okay," and she leaned against him again. "Because you know I would if you really needed me to—"

"No, no," Ken protested. Even so, he felt a flash of irritation. Here Maria was, saying that she would come to the dinner if he really needed her to—but she'd nearly bitten his head off when she'd thought he *had* needed her to. *Oh, give her a break,* Ken told himself finally. *Who can blame her for not wanting to come to that dinner? Even I'm getting sick of talking about this scholarship.*

"Everything's going to work out," Maria promised.

Ken sighed. He hoped it was true. The night before, he'd realized that the fact that his dad had felt he needed to cheat in order to get his son into a good school was really making him feel like a crappy football player, a lousy student, and a crummy human being. What if he took the scholarship but lost so much confidence that he wasn't any good on the field anymore? Ken had been waiting all day to talk to Maria about this. . . . He was glad that they were finally at lunch so they could talk, just the two of them.

They'd reached the end of the lunch line. Maria handed Ken five bucks for her food, and he took out his wallet and paid while Maria grabbed some napkins, straws, and forks. Then he headed for an empty table nearby.

He sat down and started to lift the cellophane off his sandwich. But when he looked up, he saw Maria standing beside him, still holding her tray in her hands. "Don't you want to sit with the others?" she asked.

Ken shrugged. "I don't know. I just thought we might have a little quiet time. You know, I really wanted to tell you—"

"Oh, hey!" Maria suddenly called out, waving. Ken looked across the lunchroom to see Elizabeth motioning them over to the table where Jessica and Tia were sitting.

"We'll be right there!" Maria cried. She looked back at Ken and smiled. "Is it okay?" she asked. "They're all waiting for us."

Ken stood and picked up his tray. What else could he do? "Sure," he said. "It's okay."

Reluctantly he followed Maria across the room and sat down with the others. *So much for talking things out.* He tried not to think about Maria's smile—the one that she flashed when she was truly happy . . . the one that she just gave Elizabeth. He tried very hard not to wonder how long it had been since he'd seen it.

"Hey, you guys," Elizabeth said brightly as Ken and Maria set their trays on the table. "What's going on?" She flipped her book closed and beamed at them. She was probably being obnoxiously cheerful, to tell the truth, but she couldn't help it. Exciting news always made her giddy, and Maria was practically the only person left she hadn't told yet.

Maria and Ken exchanged glances. "Okay," Maria said, looking around the table, "who slipped Liz the happy pill?"

"Don't look at *me*," Jessica said.

Tia smiled and shrugged.

"Believe me," Elizabeth said, "no pill could work this well."

"Okay, let me rephrase the question," Maria said, sitting down across from Elizabeth. She leaned toward her and said, "Who *is* he?"

Jessica gave a soft snort. "Oh, please," she said. "You're way off base now."

Elizabeth lifted her chin and said proudly, "You're looking at the newest intern on staff at the *Sweet Valley Scope.*"

"What?" Maria cried. "How? When?"

"They've got a program for seniors," Elizabeth explained. "I just interviewed yesterday, and I start tomorrow."

"That's terrific!" Maria beamed at her. Elizabeth glanced at Ken, expecting similar congratulations, but he didn't really seem to be paying attention.

"So what will you be doing there?" Maria wanted to know.

"Well, they said not to expect much at first," Elizabeth explained. "But I'm determined to write something for them. So I've got to come up with a great story. They sometimes do pieces on teens, so I thought that might be a good place to start. Any ideas?"

"How about a fashion piece?" Maria asked. "Like, the latest high-school fads. Retro versus New Age. People like that kind of thing, don't they?"

"Yeah, they do," said Elizabeth, although she knew that was miles from the piece she'd been dreaming of. Way too fluffy.

"What about dating stories?" asked Tia. "You know, how people meet and fall in love and stuff."

Elizabeth nearly laughed, seeing how Tia's eyes were practically sending off sparks. "Got anyone in particular in mind?" she teased.

"Yeah," Jessica said. "With you and Trent as the focus of the story, right? And they'll run a picture of the two of you on the cover, staring into each other's eyes, with a huge headline: Teens in Love!"

Everyone burst out laughing, and Tia blushed deeply.

"Sorry," Elizabeth said to her. "It's actually a good idea. But I was thinking of something a little newsier. They gave me some back copies of the *Scope* to take home yesterday, and I was reading an article last night on unfair practices in high-school sports."

Ken, who had been sitting totally silent, nibbling on an apple, suddenly looked over at Elizabeth. Maybe she'd triggered an idea. "Do you know of any strange things happening on our team, Ken?" she asked.

Ken shifted in his seat and gave a half smile. "Define *strange*," he said.

Maria reached over and rubbed his shoulder. "Ken wouldn't know about that, Liz," she said lightly. "And if he did, he couldn't tell you about it, or he'd have to kill you."

Elizabeth laughed, but something in Ken's reaction set off all of her reporter instincts. She took a moment to study him. Ken was staring down at the table, his face now slightly red. She knew she should just drop it, but she couldn't fight the feeling that he knew something . . . maybe something that would make a good story. . . . "So anyway, Ken," she said slowly, "you've never heard of coaches pumping kids with steroids or students having to—"

"God, Liz," Ken said with a soft laugh. "What do you think this is? A *7th Heaven* episode?"

"Oh, yeah." Jessica grinned. "Liz really identifies with that show. She's so into Matt."

"Me too," Tia said. "Major hottie."

Elizabeth glared at Jessica, annoyed that she'd

managed to steer the whole conversation off track so easily. "So anyway, Ken . . . ," she tried again.

But Ken suddenly looked at his watch. "Sorry, Liz, gotta run." He picked up his tray and his back-pack and stood up from the table. Maria stood too, but Ken gave her a quick peck on the lips. "Call you tonight," he said. Then he was gone.

The three of them looked at Maria, who slowly sank back down in her chair.

"Hey," Elizabeth said, "sorry if I said something wrong, Maria."

Maria shrugged. "It's okay. You know how those teams are—they have their code of honor and all that."

Elizabeth smiled at her but couldn't help wondering how she could stand such a touchy boyfriend. Conner had been touchy too—well, that was an understatement. Elizabeth was so glad not to have to deal with that kind of thing anymore. She had to admit her new attitude was a nice change. She only had to worry about herself now, and she liked it that way.

After lunch, though, just as they were leaving the cafeteria, Maria pulled Elizabeth off to an empty corner by the doors. "I've got to talk to you about Ken," she said softly. "He's really having a rough time."

"Oh. Really?" Elizabeth asked, trying to show concern. She forced herself to not look at her watch.

She didn't want to be rude to Maria, but she had a ton of things to read over before her shift at the *Scope* tomorrow. Besides, she didn't really want to hear about Ken's problems. After all, he hadn't been too interested in helping her with her story-idea problem just now.

"It's his scholarship," Maria said. "It's a disaster. You have no idea what's been happening."

"Hmmm," Elizabeth said. She could just imagine that Ken was freaking out over having to leave Maria to go to Michigan. *Sorry, Maria, but . . .* Big deal. "Look, I'm sorry," Elizabeth said. "I know you need to talk. But I just can't even concentrate right now. Could I call you tonight?"

"Oh," Maria said. She was clearly surprised. And hurt. "Okay. We'll talk later."

Elizabeth felt bad, but she was tired of putting her own needs on hold to talk about things like Ken's scholarship issues. *Besides, if it were Maria's problem, that would be one thing . . . but this is clearly Ken's deal.* And didn't Ken have his own friends to confide in—like his buddies on the football team that he was so protective of?

At home that night Jessica was lying facedown on her bed, trying to read her English assignment. She was supposed to be studying a particularly boring section from the textbook on grammatical syntax, and she was having trouble concentrating. Suddenly she heard a loud banging against her bedroom wall.

God, now what? she wondered. She tried covering her ears with her hands, then putting a pillow over her head, but it was no good. The pounding was nearly rattling her teeth. Finally she got up and followed the sound, which of course was coming from Elizabeth's room.

Her door was already open a crack, so Jessica pushed it until it swung wide and found Elizabeth, dressed in her nightshirt, shorts, and fuzzy slippers, hammering a nail into the wall by her desk.

"What are you *doing?*" Jessica cried. "Mom's gonna kill you. You know she hates holes in the walls."

Elizabeth glanced over her shoulder at her sister. "She hates it when people don't knock too," she said, stooping to pick up a white, plastic board from the floor. "Anyway, I put a piece of tape down first. To keep the plaster from cracking." Elizabeth took the board to the wall and hung it on the nail, then stood back to survey it. "Does that look straight to you?"

Jessica shrugged. "Close enough. What is it?" she asked.

"It's a dry-erase board. I got it on the way home from Sedona tonight. I'll need it for my *Scope* article ideas." Elizabeth pulled out a blue marker and drew three vertical lines down the board, then wrote above each of them, *Good, Okay,* and *Not Sure.*

"See?" She stared at the board intensely. "I'm going to jot down all the ideas I have for stories right up here. That way they'll be in plain view, where I can see them every day. And I can think about them while I'm studying or just hanging around, until I come up with a killer idea."

Jessica wasn't sure what to say. "Sounds like a plan," she offered.

"And I've already got a couple of things to put on the list. Remember how we talked about some topics at lunch today?"

"Uh-huh." Jessica recalled all too well how lunch had gone today. Elizabeth had pretty much interrogated Ken, trying to force him to dish out some dirt on the football team. She only hoped that Elizabeth didn't decide to do a cheerleader exposé.

Under the *Okay* heading, Elizabeth wrote *Teen Fashions;* under the *Not Sure* listing she wrote *Teen Romances.*

"What, nothing for the *Good* section yet?" Jessica joked. "You'll probably want at least one thing under there."

"Believe me, I'm working on it," Elizabeth said seriously. "And I know I'll think of something. It's just a matter of time."

Jessica walked up to the board and stared at it, shaking her head. Typically, Elizabeth was going a little overboard. "Don't you think you're getting a little worked up here?" she asked cautiously.

"Hey," Elizabeth said. "This is a serious job, and it takes time and effort." She pulled out her desk chair and sat down, then muttered, "It's not like I'm trying to think up a new cheer or something."

Instantly Jessica felt the heat rise to her face. It wasn't like Elizabeth to be so rude. *She's probably just getting freaked out over her first day at the new job tomorrow,* Jessica told herself. *Cut her some slack.*

Elizabeth sighed, then banged open the top drawer of her desk and began to sift through the contents.

"Now what are you doing?" Jessica asked, as sweetly as she could.

"Getting my supplies in order. I want everything to be right where I can grab it when inspiration hits. Not that you'd know about the importance of an orderly desk."

Jessica drew a deep breath and held it as she began to chant to herself, *I will not fight with my sister, I will not fight with my sister, I will not—*

"Jess," Elizabeth said.

Jessica forced a smile onto her face. "Yes?" she said.

"Could you please close the door on your way out?"

Jessica stared at her, slowly realizing Elizabeth wasn't kidding. She backed out of the room, saying a soft good night, and shut the door behind her. For a minute she stood in the dark hallway, feeling like she'd just had an encounter with some strange alien. To be honest, she was too confused to be mad.

Who *was* that girl back there?

To: mcdermott@cal.rr.com
From: alannaf@swiftnet.com
Subject: Long time, no you

Hey, stranger! How was your trip? I
know you have to be back by now, so
call me or something! I want to know
all about Arizona. I've never even
been there before—can you believe it?
I'm free this weekend BTW, so if
you'd like to actually see me in
person, I think I could arrange it.
Missed you—

                    Me

To: alannaf@swiftnet.com
From: mcdermott@cal.rr.com
Subject: Hey

    Sorry, buried in schoolwork this weekend. Arizona's a long, boring stretch of desert. You haven't missed a thing.

                          Conner

CHAPTER 5

One Hundred and Ten Percent

For the third time in fifteen minutes Elizabeth reached inside the gigantic beige-colored copier to pry loose a sheet of paper caught in the jumble of levers and gears. "Ouch!" she cried, then looked around, embarrassed. That was the second time she'd burned her finger on the metal plate labeled Caution: Do Not Touch. Luckily Wednesday afternoon seemed to be a slow time at the *Scope,* and no one else was in the copy room.

She hit the print button again and put her burned finger in her mouth. Apparently Joanna hadn't been kidding about the gofer aspects of this job. Elizabeth hadn't even spent one second reading or writing anything this afternoon—just unjamming copy paper, sending faxes, and answering constantly ringing phones. She listened to the monotonous *ka-chung, ka-chung* of the copier as it spit out her stapled, collated documents and thought of how totally exciting that sound would be if only it were copying an article with the byline *Elizabeth Wakefield*.

When the copy job was done, Elizabeth decided to take a minute to recharge. She headed into the break room to buy a soda and saw her supervisor, Leo Grant, sitting at a table and eating a bag of pretzels. Joanna had introduced Elizabeth to Leo, an editorial assistant at the *Scope,* when Elizabeth came in today. As far as she was concerned, he was one of the few perks of the job. With huge brown eyes rimmed with long dark lashes, curly black hair, and the whitest smile she'd ever seen, Leo was definitely the cutest supervisor she'd ever had. He'd shown Elizabeth around the office, then set her up with the odd jobs she'd been working on ever since.

"Hey." Leo flashed her that incredible smile. "How's it going?"

"Okay," Elizabeth said. She tried to smile back but knew it had to look forced.

"Ah," Leo said, his eyes narrowing. "Not quite the challenge you expected, huh?"

Elizabeth didn't want to seem negative, so she said, "No, it's fine. I mean good. Really good."

Leo nodded. "Just not Pulitzer caliber, right? Hey, I understand. It wasn't so long ago I was in your shoes, you know." Leo held out his bag of pretzels, and Elizabeth took one.

"Thanks," Elizabeth said. "Did you intern here too?"

"Oh, yeah. For my whole senior year at SVU. But by the time I graduated, I was on staff full-time. Everybody kind of pays their dues at first."

Elizabeth popped the top on her diet Coke and took a sip. "I don't mind doing that. Really. I just . . . I guess I'm just anxious to hurry up and pay them. So I can get some real experience."

Leo crumpled up his empty pretzel bag. "It's not hard," he said. "All you have to do is act like there's no job too small for you. Just give everything one hundred and ten percent. You know, show initiative." He stood up and took a jump shot at the corner garbage can with his crumpled pretzel bag. "Two points!" he cried as the bag dropped in.

"Impressive," Elizabeth said.

He waggled his eyebrows. "Well, I guess we all have our good points." His gaze held Elizabeth's for an extra moment, and she felt herself blush. Then he turned on his heel. "See you."

Elizabeth watched him leave, suddenly feeling much better. Leo was right—she had to pay her dues like everyone else. Besides, how bad could this job possibly be when her supervisor was so cute? Of course, she wouldn't dare get involved with someone at the office—this job was too important a stepping-stone for her. But it couldn't hurt to have a little, tiny flirtation with someone . . . could it?

Elizabeth marched back to her desk and grabbed her list of tasks. She crossed off all the jobs she'd already completed until the only one left was "Organize archive files for local businesses." This was one Leo had told her could wait until later, even next week sometime. Elizabeth checked her watch and saw she had forty minutes before the pep rally began. Well, she might as well show that initiative and at least get started on them.

She picked up the stack of files and took them to a large metal cabinet in the hallway where they were supposed to be stored. Once she began to sort through them, though, she saw that some of the folders were old and ripped and a few of the labels were peeling off. With Leo's words still echoing in her head, Elizabeth began reorganizing the documents—making new labels, color-coding similar jobs, and replacing old folders with fresh, new ones.

After a while she became totally absorbed in what she was doing. It wasn't so bad, doing menial, mindless work. The only problem was that it was, well . . . mindless. It let her thoughts wander. And when they wandered, they almost always found their way back to Conner.

Elizabeth had been pushing him out of her mind

ever since last semester, when they'd finally broken up for good. He'd chosen Alanna over her. She had to accept that and go on. And she *was* moving past it, getting her priorities straight for once. But it still hurt. She was just going to have to put everything she could into this job to keep him totally out of her head.

When she was nearly done with the filing, she took a minute to stretch and glance around the office. With a shock, she saw it was nearly empty. The few people who were still there were shutting off computers and packing up their briefcases.

What time was it? Elizabeth was afraid to look at her watch. Oh God, already after seven! The rally was half over. Jessica was going to kill her.

She thought of tearing out of the office and speeding over to the school. But even if she left now, she'd only be able to catch the end. She'd already missed the cheerleaders anyway, and that had been the whole point of going, hadn't it?

Elizabeth sighed, then stared at the clock another minute before turning back to her filing. *Jess will understand,* she told herself. *Won't she?*

As if in a dream, Jessica felt her feet spring off the top of Tia's shoulders, and then she was soaring into the cool evening air, higher and higher, until she hit her peak, touched the tips of her toes, and then began to fall. Instantly she let her body sink straight down, her upstretched arms making a perfect V, until she was on the ground again.

God, that felt great, Jessica thought, turning back to watch the other cheerleaders in their "human tower" do the same thing, one by one. As soon as they were all on the ground again, they went into a dance routine while the huge crowd roared its approval.

Jessica was giving one of her best performances ever; even she could tell that. The other girls on the squad were completely in sync too. The energy flowing between them was so strong that it made the evening air feel supercharged.

Still, she couldn't stop looking for Elizabeth. She stared out at the crowd, into a sea of fans all wearing red and white, and again she came up short. *She couldn't have missed this. She's just sitting behind some freakishly tall person, right?*

At last the number ended and the final roll of drums from the band pounded out the song's close. The crowd sprang to its feet and cheered. It was incredible. Jessica had never felt such a rush. She waved at Jeremy again, who was sitting with Trent in the front row, right behind the fence at the cheerleaders' section. They'd made sure to leave their Big Mesa jackets at home so the Sweet Valley students wouldn't murder them. Both of them waved back at her, and Jessica threw her arm around Tia, pulling her close in a tight little hug. "We did it," Jessica said. "Was that awesome or what?"

"Amazing," Tia said. She was staring at Trent, though, so Jessica wasn't exactly sure what she was referring to. But who cared? Right here, right now, everything was perfect.

Except that she still hadn't found her sister. She and Tia, along with the rest of the cheerleaders, left the field now and took their seats in the cheering section where they would stay until the end of the rally. Jessica watched as Coach Riley walked onto the field and began to announce the first-string football players. He was giving medals of appreciation to everyone on the team for the great season they'd had this year.

Ken's name was called first of course, and he ran onto the field and gave a quick wave, then stood with his head down while his teammates joined him one by one. Ken seemed totally wrecked these days. Thank goodness he was with someone great like Maria and not with that nightmare Melissa Fox anymore.

The thought of Maria immediately brought Elizabeth to mind again, and Jessica turned around in her seat to look for her as Coach Riley wrapped up his speech. If Elizabeth wasn't here by now, she was pretty much going to miss everything.

She must have had to work late, Jessica thought, her spirits sinking despite the energy in the air. It wasn't so awful that she'd been stood up. Jessica realized work was work. But that nagging worry was creeping through her again. She thought about Elizabeth in the library, with all those books around her. And then the lunch with Ken and how rude she'd been last night. And now this. *And people think I'm intense,* Jessica thought.

Half an hour later, when it was all over, Jessica walked off the field with Tia, knowing for sure now that Elizabeth hadn't made it at all. If she had come, she would definitely be standing at the fence with Jeremy and Trent, who were waiting for them to come through the gate.

"Oh, man," Jeremy said when she and Tia reached the gate. "That was amazing!" He wrapped her in a huge hug and gave her lips a light kiss. "I can't believe you didn't land on your butt!"

She laughed, shoving him away. He fell into Trent and Tia, who broke apart, their own kiss interrupted.

"Hey, you guys!" Jessica heard someone shout. She turned to see Maria waving wildly at them, her other arm around Ken's waist. She hurried over, half dragging Ken behind her. "You were great," Maria said breathlessly. "I never knew the squad was so tight, Jess. And didn't Ken look adorable out there?"

She pecked him on the cheek. Ken kept his eyes on the ground.

"It *was* amazing, wasn't it?" Jessica was beaming. She couldn't help it.

"Yeah," Ken said, wearing that same dismal look again. "You guys were great. You ready to go, Maria?"

Jessica frowned at him. "Oh, you're not leaving already, are you? We should all go somewhere. Celebrate a little."

"How about Casey's?" Trent suggested. "I could use a milk shake."

"Sounds good to me," Tia agreed.

They all looked at Ken, who was staring at Maria without saying anything. Finally she put her hand on his shoulder, then turned to Jessica and said, "You guys have fun. We really need to get going."

"Yeah, see you," Ken said as he took Maria's hand and headed for the parking lot.

Jessica stood staring after them for a moment.

"Weird," Jeremy said finally.

"*Very* weird," Jessica agreed. Ken was acting strange. Elizabeth was acting strange.

Maybe there was something in the water.

Now what? Evan looked around at the few people sipping lattes and reading magazines on the couches at HOJ. He'd meant to get there about ten minutes early, to give himself time to settle into one of the cushy, velvet booths and to think about what he was going to say to Jade. But somehow he'd overachieved. He'd gotten there almost twenty minutes early and had made the mistake of choosing a table directly across from the entrance. Now he was stuck there, staring at the doors with nothing to do. *This is not the way to look ultracool in front of Jade,* he realized.

Luckily he had his backpack from school with him. He opened up his English notebook and started to scribble a few stupid drawings on the page. Anything to look like he was busy with something other than door watching.

Of course, the minute the bell over the doors jingled, he jerked his head up to see if it was Jade. It wasn't. But it *was* someone he knew. Tommy Puett, his old buddy from El Carro, walked in with a pretty blue-eyed girl. Tommy immediately spotted Evan and headed for his table.

"Plummer!" Tommy cried. "I thought this place was strictly for caff addicts. They don't let swimmers drink coffee, do they?"

Evan held up his coffee cup and pointed to it. "Chai tea."

"So you're the guy who gets the chai tea. I always wondered who ordered that stuff." Tommy chuckled, then gestured toward the girl. "Do you know Roni?"

Evan was just about to say, "I don't think so," when Roni cut him off.

"Oh, we go way back," she said, tossing her wavy, shoulder-length hair. "We were in Mrs. Farley's ninth-grade math class together."

Evan silently thanked fate for letting Roni say that before he made an idiot out of himself. *How could I have forgotten?* "That's right," he said. "Mrs. Farley—we used to call her Jiffy Pop because she was always in such a hurry to give us quizzes. I nearly flunked her class."

"No kidding." She shook her head, then looked at Tommy. "Evan used to borrow my notes almost every day."

"Huh," said Tommy. "No wonder he almost flunked."

"Shut *up*," Roni said, laughing. Before Evan knew what was happening, she slid into the booth and was sitting right next to him. "Okay if we join you?"

Evan opened his mouth, but he couldn't think of any way to say no without offending them. "Uh, sure," he said. "Have a seat."

Tommy sat down across from him. Somehow Roni had scooted so close to Evan that their legs were touching. Now she nudged him with her elbow. "I can't believe we're running into you, Evan. Your name just came up the other day when I was talking to Nikki Waters, and I was saying that I thought you'd fallen off the end of the earth."

Evan pressed his lips together. *That's funny,* he thought, *because I'd totally forgotten you existed.* "Yeah," he said finally. "It's weird how stuff like that happens." Now that he studied her more closely, she was starting to look familiar. But she'd definitely changed a lot since freshman year. Then again, who hadn't?

"Exactly," Roni agreed eagerly. "So tell Tommy about that cute little nickname you had for me back at El Carro, Ev," she said.

Evan raised his eyebrows. He didn't want to seem rude, but he had absolutely no idea what she was talking about. "Uh, why don't you tell him?"

Roni smiled and turned to Tommy. "Evan used to call me 'Bonehead.' Isn't that right?" she asked, flashing a grin at Evan.

Oh, man! Evan stifled a groan. When he was in the ninth grade, he'd gone through a seriously obnoxious phase in which he called everyone Bonehead. Did Roni really think that he'd made that up especially for her? He felt like apologizing for being such a geek—but clearly Roni thought it was cute. *Ah, jeez. Well, I guess there's no need to enlighten her now,* he decided.

"Hey, by the way," Tommy said. "We're not butting in on you, are we?"

"Actually," Evan admitted, "I'm supposed to be meeting somebody." He checked his watch. "She's a little late."

"You have a *date?*" Roni cried. "Shut *up!* I'm way jealous." She batted her eyes and twirled a piece of hair around her finger. Something about the pose struck Evan as funny, but he couldn't tell if she was being serious or what, so he didn't dare laugh.

"Who is she?" Tommy asked. "Anyone I know?"

"I don't think so," Evan said. "She's just a friend."

Roni tilted her head to look at him. "Just a friend? Well, then, no problem. We're all friends, right?" She picked up a menu and began to look it over. "They have desserts here, don't they? I could go for something chocolate."

"You always want chocolate," Tommy said. "How come you don't weigh two hundred pounds?"

"Clean living," Roni deadpanned. She craned her neck to look around. "Where's the waiter anyway?" she asked. "Evan, you want something?"

But Evan was eyeing the door again. Suddenly he wasn't feeling so well.

"Yeah," he said. "I'd like something." But he knew that what he needed wasn't on the menu.

"That was such a rush," Melissa said to Will as they walked to his car after the rally. "We were all completely on the same track for once. Even Little Miss Wakefield had her act together for a change."

Will felt her loop her arm through his as they walked. He decided not to say anything about the Jessica remark. Melissa had done a great job today, and there was no need to start a battle that he knew he couldn't win. The two of them were heading out to dinner, and he wanted the evening to go smoothly.

"You were great out there," he said to her. "Best moves on the field."

Melissa smiled up at him. Her face was still flushed with heat, and she looked even more beautiful than usual. "Thanks," she said, and gave his arm a squeeze.

No matter how long they'd been together, that same little warmth always spread through him when she looked up at him like that. On impulse he stopped walking, wrapped her in his arms, and kissed her deeply.

"Wow," she said when he pulled back slightly. "What was that for?"

"I don't know," he said softly. "For being pretty. And for not saying anything else about Ken. I really appreciate that, Liss."

Melissa toyed with a button on his shirt. "I know," she said. "I thought about it, and I decided I wouldn't want to mess up your job or anything. I wouldn't do that to you, Will." Then she looked up at him, and her blue eyes turned to steel. "But I want you to know that I'm only doing this for you. Not for him. As far as Ken's concerned, I don't give a damn if the whole world finds out. In fact, I hope they do."

He kissed her forehead, then started walking again, pulling her along beside him. Then, as if Will had somehow summoned him, he spotted Ken standing next to his Trooper with Maria. He tried to steer Melissa away before she could see them, but it was too late.

"Well," she said. "Speak of the devil and the devil's girlfriend." She immediately started to head toward them.

"Don't," he said, grabbing her hand. "Melissa, let's just go. . . ."

"Why?" she asked, shaking him off. "I can at least speak to a couple of my classmates, can't I?" Before he could respond, she broke away from him and strolled over to Ken's car. "Hi, you two," she called in a high, singsong voice.

Ken and Maria both turned and stared at her, clearly startled by her friendly tone.

"Did you have fun at the rally?" Melissa asked them. To anyone who didn't know her, that voice might actually sound sincere. But Will could hear the edge behind it—and he knew what it meant.

Maria stared across the roof of the car at Ken, who was still fumbling with his keys. *They're just going to ignore her,* Will realized with relief.

But Melissa was relentless. "I *hope* you had fun today," she sang out. "Really, I mean it. You should have all the fun you can now. I mean, before the whole town realizes their star football player really isn't such a star after all."

Will winced.

Ken had the car unlocked now. "It's open, Maria," he said.

But Maria ignored him and threw Melissa a look that would melt steel. "Why don't you just mind your own business for once?" she said.

Will reached out and grabbed Melissa's arm, but she shook it loose again and stepped away from him. "If I were you, Maria, I'd worry less about me and more about your grades. I'd hate to see you lose that Senate scholarship."

Now Ken wheeled to face her. "Maria's had a perfect average since the sixth grade," he growled.

Melissa's eyes flicked over Ken, as if she was sizing him up. "We're not in the sixth grade anymore," she said coldly. "In case you haven't noticed, things have gotten a little more challenging. Right, Maria?"

Ken was staring at Maria. Her mouth flew open,

but then she shut it quickly and glared at Melissa.

"Sorry," Melissa went on, "but I couldn't help catching a glimpse of that giant red C on your last French quiz." She shook her head. "I don't see how you can keep the scholarship with grades like that. . . . Then again, maybe there's someone you can pay off."

Maria looked like she was getting ready to blast Melissa off the ground with some raging comeback, and Will waited expectantly, almost hoping she would. But after throwing another angry stare at her, Maria simply opened the car door. "Let's just go," she said to Ken. Then she climbed in.

"Melissa, come *on*," Will said, grabbing her arm again. This time he locked his grip on her and managed to drag her away. "Sorry," he called out to Ken and Maria as he pulled her away from them.

By the time they reached his car, Will's hands were shaking so badly that he couldn't get the door open. He couldn't remember the last time he'd been so furious. Finally he managed to unlock his side. He got in and slammed the door, feeling like his head was going to explode. After a minute he hit the button to unlock Melissa's side. She calmly got in beside him, then flipped down the visor and checked her makeup in the mirror.

He gripped the steering wheel, trying to calm himself before he spoke. "What was that?" he said finally.

Melissa turned toward him, that look of total innocence on her face. "I didn't say anything Maria doesn't already know. And I haven't told anyone else, Will. I promise." She reached out and stroked his arm. "Look," she said. Her voice was deep and husky, thick with emotion. "I know you don't hold a grudge against those two. But I still do. And I'm not going to stop feeling the way I feel just because you say so."

Will sat and stared at the dashboard for a few seconds, then finally started the car. She had a good point. He couldn't control her every move or tell her how to feel about people.

As he backed out, he suddenly remembered his last conversation with Ken. Will had urged him to take the scholarship, and he still felt like he should. But he had to admit, if Ken turned it down, his own life would be a lot easier. Melissa wouldn't have anything on Ken then, and Will could stop worrying that a bomb was going to go off any minute.

Jessica Wakefield

Why is my life always <u>almost</u> perfect?

Like right now. I'm dating an awesome guy, Tia's dating Trent and we're all going to have tons of fun together, and school is under control . . . but now Liz is acting weird. I'm telling you, there's always something in my life that's totally out of whack. Like, if things at school are good, my love life is in the toilet. And if my love life is going well, Sweet Valley has an earthquake or something.

Maybe I shouldn't even try to make this Liz thing better. Maybe I'll only end up making something else worse. But how am I supposed to sit by and let my sister become The Hermit of the Newsroom?

Just please, God, no more earthquakes.

CHAPTER

Whiplash

6

Jade brushed off the front of her dress as she stepped up to the House of Java entrance. She was wearing a black sundress that tended to catch every little piece of lint. Noticing her reflection in the glass doors, she smoothed down her hair one last time. *Am I overdressed?* she wondered. Knowing Evan, the answer was probably yes. But she'd tried on so many outfits that she'd finally run out of time and had to go with the last thing she had on. Now she was feeling self-conscious, and it was so unfamiliar and strange that she had to fight the urge to run away. *What's the matter with me?* Jade wondered. *I never act like this.*

She gripped the door handle firmly, twisted it, and stepped inside, scanning the place for Evan. It didn't take long to find him. There he was, sitting dead center in a booth on the far wall. He was adorable in a brown shirt that made his hair look even darker. And with him, Jade realized with a sudden lurch, were a guy and a girl she'd never seen before.

Her heart seemed to drop into her stomach. *Oh God, he brought his* friends? Up until that point Jade had never really allowed herself to think of this get-together with Evan as a date. But now that it clearly *wasn't* a date, she found herself blinking hard behind her sunglasses, fighting back tears.

She stood still, hoping to breathe again at some point. Her palms broke out in a sweat, and for a second she actually considered backing out the door. But in the next moment Evan saw her and waved her over to the table.

She managed to smile and made her way across the room. "Hi," she said to him. "Sorry I'm late." She shoved her sunglasses up onto the top of her head, hoping that her eyes didn't look too watery.

"No problem," Evan said. "You look great. Guys, this is Jade. This is Tommy and Roni. They're old friends of mine from El Carro."

"Hey," Jade said, giving them both a little wave and doing her best to appear casual. But she hadn't sat down yet and wasn't sure which of these people to sit beside, and it was making her feel awkward. Just then Roni reached down on the floor to get her purse. After glancing inside it, she set it back down beside her, on the seat closest to Jade.

Well, that settles that. Jade scooted in beside

Tommy, her face already feeling frozen in the fake smile she'd plastered there.

"So," Roni said, pointing from Jade to Evan, "what's the story with you two?"

Jade glanced at Evan, slightly mortified. Thankfully, just at that moment the waiter came over to take her order.

"I'll have an iced cappuccino," Jade said after a quick glance at the menu. She saw that everyone else was already having something to eat—a piece of chocolate cake for Roni, a giant cookie for Tommy, and an oat-bran muffin for Evan—but Jade just wanted something she could gulp down quickly. *I'm going to blow out of here so fast, Evan'll have whiplash,* she thought.

When the waiter had gone, Jade turned to Tommy. "So you two go to Big Mesa now?" she asked.

"Yeah." He shrugged. "It's okay, but . . ."

"Oh, it can't even compare," Roni said, looping one finger through her necklace. "El Carro was so much more modern. Even the basketball court at Big Mesa is in bad shape. It took me a week of practices just to figure out where all the dead spots on the floor are."

"Oh," Jade said warily, "you play basketball?"

"Yep," Roni said, with a small smile. "Forward."

"Hey, that's Jade's position," Evan said. Jade

looked at him. Was it her imagination, or did he say it with a certain amount of pride?

"In-ter-es-ting." Roni eyed Jade even more intensely. "We're playing each other this weekend, aren't we?"

"You're kidding!" Tommy grinned.

"Afraid not," Jade said, tracing her finger along the table. *God, could this get any worse?*

Luckily the waiter appeared and placed Jade's order in front of her. Evan glanced over at her, wearing this half smile that she swore seemed almost apologetic. Or was he just feeling sorry for her? She couldn't tell. Jade picked up her iced cappuccino and downed half of it in one gulp.

"So, Jade," Roni said as she dug her fork into her piece of cake, "do you play any other sports?"

"I was cheering in the fall," Jade said. She took another monster swig of cappuccino.

Roni's mouth twisted into a smile. "That's not exactly a sport."

"It is the way they do it at SVH," Evan put in.

"Hmmm," Roni said. Then she looked at Tommy and said, "Blue goulash." Tommy burst out laughing. Jade had no idea what that meant, so she looked over at Evan for a translation. He gave her a little search-me shrug.

Jade was getting annoyed. "What does that mean?" she demanded.

"Oh, nothing," Roni said nonchalantly. "It's just something we say at Big Mesa."

Great, now we're getting into in jokes, Jade thought. *Soon this girl and her little friend will be speaking in code.* Jade sneaked another look at Evan. *These guys are his friends?* she wondered. All at once the thought of staying even a minute longer made her crazy. On impulse she looked at her watch. "Oh God, I'm late!" she said. She knew she sounded like she was lying, but she didn't care. "I'm sorry," she went on. "But I really have to run now. I'm meeting somebody."

Evan's mouth dropped opened a bit, like he was going to say something. But then he shut it again as his eyes fell to the table. Jade couldn't tell for sure, but he almost looked disappointed. Anyway, she didn't have time to think about it. She had to get out of here before she lost it, big time.

"Nice meeting you two," she said. "Bye, Evan." She forced a last dazzling smile at them all, then sprinted from the restaurant, her heart pounding all the way out to her car. Jade opened the door, dropped inside, and slammed the door behind her. She leaned her head against the steering wheel. She suddenly had a splitting headache, and the cool steering wheel felt good against her forehead. After a few minutes she looked up, catching a glimpse of her eyes in the rearview mirror. *Well, you just got it all wrong,* she thought. *Obviously Evan wants to keep you around as a friend. And that's all.*

She started the car, realizing that in spite of everything, she was actually feeling a pang of guilt for lying about having to meet someone. She hated lying. But she had to have an excuse to leave right away. And she had to make it seem like she had dressed up for something.

And I have to seem like I have some kind of life, don't I?

"Okay, she's driven, but she's also very dependable," Jessica was saying as she ran her plastic spoon in circles over her double-fudge chocolate yogurt, trying to scrape up all the sprinkles. Casey's was packed, as if the entire pep-rally crowd had all had the same craving for ice cream. She, Jeremy, Tia, and Trent were squeezed around a tiny white table near the back. "Usually. I just can't believe she would blow me off this way," Jessica fumed.

"Come on, Jess. Is it really such a big deal?" Jeremy asked. "Just let her do her thing. She'll go nuts over this internship for a while, and then she'll calm down." He scooped up a huge mouthful of mint chocolate chip with whipped cream.

Jessica frowned. "But you didn't see her in her

room last night, banging on the wall like a crazy person and talking about how this dry-erase board was going to change her life."

Tia giggled. "I think I saw an infomercial like that."

Jessica rolled her eyes. "I know it sounds funny, but this is serious. You don't know how she can get about things."

Trent, who had been quietly sipping his milk shake, turned to Jessica. "Sounds serious to me," he said. "I mean, when someone who's usually dependable stands you up, you have to wonder what's up with them."

"*Thank* you," Jessica said, pointing her hand at Trent. She raised her eyebrows at Jeremy as if to say, *See?*

"You know, maybe she should do something with the four of us sometime," Trent suggested. "I mean, we could help take her mind off this new job a little."

Jessica could have hugged him. "Of course!" she cried. "That's it!"

"What's it?" Jeremy asked.

Jessica beamed at him. "We all have such a great time together because we're such close friends, right? So why don't we just expand our group a little? We could set Liz up with someone you guys know from Big Mesa." She looked at Trent, then Jeremy, then Trent again. "We could do it this Friday! Isn't that brilliant?"

"Wait a minute," Jeremy said. "I'm not really into fix ups."

"Yeah, Jess," Tia said. "It can get messy. What if things don't work out?"

Jessica heaved an exasperated sigh. "Well, then, the world won't end, will it?"

Jeremy shook his head. "I don't know," he said. "Don't most people hate blind dates? I know I would."

"*Liz* sure would," Tia agreed.

Jessica sighed again. They just didn't get it. "Well, we're not going to *tell* her it's a blind date."

"What?" Jeremy cried. "Oh, now I'm totally against this. You can't *trick* her into going out with someone."

"Liz would kill you," Tia said.

"Come *on*, Tee." Trent shook his head. "Liz won't mind as long as she likes the guy. And it won't be a high-stress thing . . . we'll just be a bunch of friends hanging out. If they don't hit it off, no big loss."

Jessica smiled at him, thankful someone was on her side. "Great," she said. "So who can we set her up with?"

"Well, let me think. . . ." Trent played with his straw for a second, then said, "David Dollinger?"

"Too short," Jeremy said.

"Michael Taff?"

Jeremy rolled his eyes. "Too high on himself."

"Okay." Trent shrugged. "Jeff Heintz?"

Jeremy stared at his friend. "The guy wears a *cape.*"

Trent turned to Jessica. "I thought your sister was an arty writer type," he said.

"Not that arty," Jessica replied. "Think cute, smart, and available."

"Okay," Trent said. "How about Jason Dorman? He's blond and blue-eyed—"

"And he's got a girlfriend," Jeremy said, frowning. "Look, let me just go on record with this one more time. I really don't think we should do this. People should just stay out of each other's love lives."

Jessica stared at him, then turned back to Trent. "So who else do you know?" Jessica asked him. Then she turned back to Jeremy. "Come on," she urged. "*Think!*"

Jeremy looked at Tia, who shrugged and smiled. "Telling Jessica to stay out of people's love lives is like telling Christina Aguilera to stick with her natural hair color," Tia said. "You should know better."

With a sigh Jeremy threw his arm around Jessica. "Okay, you win. There's got to be somebody. We'll keep thinking."

On impulse Jessica leaned over and kissed his cheek. "Thanks," she whispered.

"You know," Tia put in suddenly, "the real obstacle won't be us. It'll be Liz. You'll never convince her to come out Friday night."

Jessica frowned, then stared down at a spot on the table. "Yeah," she said. "That's true."

"I mean, if she missed the rally . . . ," Tia said.

Wait, that's it! Jessica realized. The thought made her so happy, she nearly clapped. Elizabeth had missed the rally. She had ditched her sister and broken her promise to be there. Jessica smiled smugly. "No problem," she said. "I know just the motivation to get Liz to come."

The three of them looked at her blankly.

"Don't you know? It's the one-word charm," she said. "Guilt."

She's not coming back, Evan told himself. *So stop staring at the doors, you jerk.* He shifted around in his seat, turning away from the HOJ entrance and more toward Roni, who was still yammering nonstop about something—basketball now, he realized. He tried to listen, but his thoughts kept drifting back to Jade and that weird little encounter they'd just had.

He couldn't believe she had made plans with someone else when they were supposed to be spending time together. Why had she done that? Was she deliberately trying to hurt him? Maybe so. That would explain why she was looking so extra gorgeous. She wanted to rub his face in it.

But who could she be seeing? He wanted to kick himself for not asking, but he'd been taken so off guard. After all, she was supposed to be on a date with *him! Oh, man, this exciting little outing sure turned into a total suck-a-thon.*

"Hey!" Roni cried. She waved her hand in front of his face. "Yoo-hoo. Anybody home?"

Evan snapped to attention. "What?" he said. "Oh, sorry. I guess I zoned for a minute." He realized he'd been staring at the doors again.

Roni leaned toward Evan, a smirk playing on her lips. "Well, if you were daydreaming about *me*, of course," she said, "then I guess I can forgive you."

Evan forced a polite laugh, then said, "I just . . . I've just got a lot on my mind right now."

Roni slapped the table in a decisive gesture. "Well, then that settles it," she said. "You're coming out on Friday night. You need to get your mind on more important things. Like sports."

"Friday night?" Evan asked.

Roni stared at him, then at Tommy. "Do you believe this guy?"

Tommy grinned at Evan. "I think she just asked you to come to her game on Friday."

"Oh," Evan said. *Friday? Game?* His mind was still a jumble. Finally the pieces began to move, then clicked into place. "Oh, your basketball game!"

"Of course!" Roni said. "Want to come cheer me on like a true El Carro alumni?"

Evan picked up his napkin and started to tear it into thin shreds. "Well," he said, "Fridays are pretty busy for me."

"Look," Roni said, "I know you're not really into sports all that much, except for swimming, obviously. But it'll be fun—we're playing Sweet Valley."

"Yeah," Evan said absently. He wadded the shreds of napkin into a tiny ball and rolled it along the table, trying to think. Well, it's not like he had any other plans. And it *was* a Friday night, after all, not exactly a study night. "Okay," he said finally. "I guess I can make it. Thanks."

Roni beamed at him. "Great," she said. "And you can help me by watching my game and taking notes. It shouldn't be too boring for you."

Of course it won't be boring, he thought. Basketball was cool. Besides, he'd probably see some old friends at the game. That would be good. And of course it was *girls'* basketball, so there was always that advantage. Yep, those were all solid reasons for going.

And then there was that other reason, of course. The one he wouldn't let himself think about.

Oh, no, he wouldn't be thinking about Jade at all.

* * *

God, how did I get into this? Ken wondered as he slouched in his seat at the newest Latin restaurant in town, Flamenco. He glanced around the table at the intense faces of his father, Hank Krubowski, and Coach Garrett, all of them hunched over their plates, anxiously talking about football like they were planning strategy for the next Super Bowl.

"What's this I hear about you switching to more of a running game next year?" Ken's father asked.

"Well, that's probably an overstatement," Coach Garrett said. He was a solidly built man with blond hair streaked gray at the temples and lines at his eyes that crinkled when he smiled. "I plan to have a balanced attack between the run and the pass."

"I'm glad to hear that. I wouldn't want you to waste my son's talents." Ken's father laughed, then his face went serious again. "You know one of Ken's best strengths is reading defenses—"

Ken turned away and began to look around the restaurant again, sick of hearing his father promise how he would single-handedly take Michigan to the national championship. He gazed at the flickering candles on the tables and the dimly lit bar across the room. None of this felt right. Even this restaurant was way too elegant for him. He wished he was at Enzo's, staring over the table at Maria's pretty face instead of looking at these guys. In front of him sat his plate, nearly untouched. He had hardly eaten a thing. He pushed a little of his salad around with his fork to make it look like a few bites were missing. What kind of lettuce *was* that anyway?

"So you think he'll have to be redshirted next year?" his father asked Coach Garrett.

"Not necessary," he said. "I plan on getting him out there on the field as soon as possible. See what he can do against the big boys right off the bat." Garrett gave Ken a warm smile, then took another bite of his fettuccini.

Ken had to admit the coach seemed like a great guy—really straightforward and honest. He'd already described the great facilities at Michigan and had gone on to talk about both the strengths of the team and the places where it needed some improvement. Of course, he failed to mention the winters there that could freeze your tongue to the roof of your mouth until spring.

"See, Ken, redshirt status is generally given to most first-year students," said Krubowski, pointing at Ken with his fork. "It means that although they're on scholarship and they're allowed to live and practice with the team, most of them don't actually play until their sophomore year."

"I know what redshirt means," Ken said darkly. He liked that guy less every time he was around him.

But if he did decide to play for Michigan, he knew he wouldn't have to deal with him anyway, thanks to the deal his dad had arranged for Krubowski to take over as assistant coach at Southern Cal next year.

Coach Garrett cleared his throat. "Our approach to running the team is that everybody gets a shot, and we get the most out of all of our players. Everyone gets on the field to contribute as soon as they're ready."

Ken's father placed his hand on Ken's shoulder. "Sounds good, doesn't it, son?" His eyebrows were arched in an expression that said both, "Isn't that great?" and "Show some enthusiasm or I'm going to kill you."

"See, the thing about playing for Michigan is," Coach Garrett said, "it's not just your teammates who are behind you. It's a hundred years of great football tradition and a hundred thousand fans in the biggest stadium in the country." He leaned across the table toward Ken and said in a low voice, "I can't describe to you exactly what that means, Ken. You just have to be a part of it to understand."

Man, this guy is good. The words he said and the gravelly tone of his voice actually made the hair on the back of Ken's neck stand up. And Ken had to admit that a hundred thousand fans sounded really cool.

"I'm sure you know we have a really good team coming back next year," the coach continued. "We lost only six starters—two of whom went to the NFL, I might add—but what you might not know is that we have a lot of great recruits joining the team next year with you. I'm counting on next season to be one of our best ever. This team is going to be a real powerhouse for the next few years."

Ken nodded at the coach. He realized he'd scooted forward in his chair. This man literally had him on the edge of his seat.

"So Ken," Krubowski said, "you've hardly said a word tonight. Why don't you tell us what you think about coming to our school?"

"He thinks he'd be nuts not to," Ken's father said, eyeing his son over the top of his wineglass before taking a sip.

Ken stared at him, trying not to let his resentment show, but Krubowski merely chuckled. "That right, Ken? Or is your old man just giving you a hard time?"

Ken looked down at his plate. He knew Krubowski probably hadn't meant to put him on the spot with his dad. Of course, the guy had no idea Ken knew about the deal they'd cut. Still, Ken didn't know how to answer him.

Luckily he didn't have to since the coach broke in just then. "Come on, you two," he said in a low voice. "Give this young man a chance to think things over." He leaned across the table again and handed Ken an official-looking envelope. "This is your letter of intent, Ken. You take this home, sleep on it, and talk things over with your dad. Then you let us know what you decide on Friday. Okay?"

Ken felt so relieved and so grateful to the coach for stepping in, he had to stop himself from just picking it up and signing it now. But he knew that wasn't even allowed. There was some rule that a letter of intent couldn't be signed in front of the prospective coach. He guessed that nobody wanted to be accused of pressuring players into joining their team . . . even if that was what they were doing. "Thanks," Ken said as he took the envelope. "I'll let you know by Friday. I promise." He glanced at his father just in time to see him give an almost imperceptible nod.

Oh, well. At least he had two more days to decide. But playing football for Coach Garrett didn't seem like such a bad prospect at all. Ken was starting to think again about how Will and maybe even his own father were right—he'd be crazy to turn all this down.

All of a sudden Ken felt hungry. He picked up the dessert menu and began to look it over.

"Great idea," Coach Garrett said. He stared at the menu for a moment, then shook his head. "Decisions, decisions," he said to Ken. "I can never make up my mind."

Tell me about it, Ken thought.

Evan Plummer

Top-five possible reasons
Jade blew me off tonight:

5. She had a date.
4. She just wants to be friends.
3. She was afraid of spilling coffee on
   her good clothes.
2. Her favorite TV show was on.
1. <u>She had a date?</u>

CHAPTER 7

Exploding Conscience

Elizabeth stared hard at the problem in front of her, trying to command her brain to come up with the right formula. It was Thursday and the second time this week she'd ditched lunch in favor of the library. She just had to get this math homework done if she was going to work her shift at Sedona this afternoon. What was the *formula* for this one?

Her brain was on hold lately. Except when it came to the *Scope* anyway. She'd still been trying to come up with just the right story idea, and thoughts of potential topics were reeling through her head at all hours. Even now she was thinking about it, she realized. She gripped her pencil more tightly and tried again to focus on the problem.

Suddenly a voice broke into her thoughts. "I figured I'd find you here." Elizabeth looked up to see Maria standing by her table. Oh God, *Maria!* She'd called when Elizabeth was at work yesterday, but by the time Elizabeth had gotten home, she'd been too dead to call her back.

"Hey, there," Elizabeth said.

"Got a minute, Liz?" Maria's eyes looked heavy, as if she desperately needed a nap.

"Of course! I'm so sorry I didn't get a chance to call you back last night. . . ."

"It's okay. I know you're swamped."

"Sit down," Elizabeth said, pulling out a chair. "Maria, you look exhausted."

"I've been up half the night studying." Maria yawned, then sat down sideways in her chair and leaned as close to Elizabeth as possible. "Liz, this can't wait any longer," she said softly. "I've got to tell somebody or I'll lose it."

The urgency in Maria's voice sent a chill up Elizabeth's spine. "What's wrong?" she asked.

Maria took a deep breath, then said, "Ken's father bribed the Michigan coach to get Ken on the football team."

Elizabeth almost started to laugh until she saw the dead seriousness in Maria's eyes. "Oh my God," she whispered. "How do you know?"

Maria closed her eyes and placed her fingers gently over the lids. "Will overheard him talking to the scout at the championship game. Mr. Matthews got the Michigan scout an assistant-coaching job in exchange for Ken's scholarship."

Elizabeth couldn't speak. In a flash she replayed all the times she'd seen Ken lately, especially the other day at lunch, and suddenly it all made sense. Of course he was acting weird! Who *wouldn't* be?

"Oh God," Elizabeth said again. "Poor Ken."

"It's driving him crazy, Liz. I just don't know what to do for him."

Elizabeth couldn't say anything for a minute, she was so stunned by the news. *A bribe!* It was like something that would happen in a bad B movie or an after-school special, not in real life.

"Last night Ken stayed really late at my house, and I tried to talk to him and be there for him," Maria said. "But he was so depressed, he just sat there, staring into space. He wants me there all the time, but it's like *he's* not even there. And meanwhile I'm freaking out over my classes, Liz. I mean, with this Senate scholarship and all, talk about pressure. Just yesterday I was trying to study for . . ."

Elizabeth nodded sympathetically, listening as Maria continued to talk. She tried hard to focus on what her friend was saying, but in her head the wheels began to turn.

What a great story.

The thought leaped into her mind and wouldn't leave, even when she tried to chase it away.

What a totally, completely, unbelievably perfect article for the Scope! *A major exposé!*

Effortlessly the details began to form. Which slant would work best for the piece, and how she could lay out all the facts? Of course, first she'd have to come up with the perfect way to pitch the idea to Joanna. It would definitely be tricky. Ken was her friend, after all, and she didn't want to make things any worse for him. But a story like this could take her to the top a lot faster than color coding files! Maybe she could just do a generic piece investigating college-sports scholarships in general and then mention . . .

"Liz, hel-lo!" Maria waved her hand in front of Elizabeth's face, looking annoyed. "Are you listening to me?"

"Sorry," Elizabeth said. "I was just thinking." She shook her head, trying to refocus her thoughts. *Maria. Ken. Trouble.* She was supposed to be helping. "It seems like you're doing all the right things," she said. "You're there for Ken, but you're not telling him how to decide. I really think that's the most important thing you can do for him now."

Maria sighed, then folded her hands together and put them under her chin. "I just wish it would all go away."

"Yeah," Elizabeth agreed. "I know."

"What really sucks is that Melissa had to find out about it. You just know she's going to tell the whole world." Maria groaned.

Elizabeth bit her lip and looked away from her friend. "Maybe not," she said. "And anyway, it would die down quickly even if she did. People tend to forget about things in a hurry."

Maria stared at her, her eyes suddenly huge. "Are you *kidding?*" she demanded. "If anyone found out about this, Ken would be in serious trouble. And his father could go to *jail.* This isn't the kind of thing people forget about."

Elizabeth stared down at her math problem. The numbers seemed to shift and chase each other across the page.

"Anyway," Maria said. "Thanks for listening, at least."

Elizabeth looked at her and smiled weakly. "No problem," she said.

Maria pushed back her chair. "I'll see you later," she said.

Elizabeth watched her walk out of the library, the little pang of guilt that had been gnawing at her insides now starting to eat right through her. How could she possibly write an article like this? Ken would never speak to her again. And *Maria.* God, Maria would end their friendship, right then and there. And Elizabeth wouldn't blame her.

No, it was too big a risk. She gathered her books and stuffed them into her backpack, resolving to take this one to her grave if she had to.

And then she saw Melissa go by in the hallway.

Wait a minute. The wheels in Elizabeth's brain started turning furiously again. If Melissa already knew about this, then it was probably just a matter of time before she let the news drop in a big way. Why should she let Melissa scoop her? And at least if Elizabeth told the story, it would be the truth!

Besides, she reminded herself for probably the hundredth time that week, *it's all about me now.* And as obnoxious as that sounded, she was determined to follow through.

Elizabeth grabbed her math notebook back out of her pack and flipped to a clean page. Still walking down the hall, she started to scribble some notes on the story. She would work on the proposal tonight and give it to Joanna right after school tomorrow.

There was no backing out of it now.

"I can't believe she didn't show up for lunch again," Jessica said to Tia. They were sitting in French, their last class of the day, waiting for Elizabeth to arrive and plotting how to handle it when she did. "She keeps disappearing—who does she think she is? David Blaine? Do you know I haven't seen her since this time yesterday?"

Tia closed the compact she'd been looking into and stared at Jessica. "How did that happen?" she asked. "You two *live* together."

"Supposedly. But by the time I got back from Casey's last night, she was sound asleep. Mom said Liz totally crashed after she got home from work. And when I got up this morning, she'd already left for school." Jessica lifted her eyebrows. "She said she had to get to the library early, so Dad gave her a ride."

Tia shook her head and smiled. "Maybe she's avoiding you."

"She's avoiding something," Jessica agreed, "but I don't think it's me."

Tia tilted her head and asked, "What do you mean?"

Jessica frowned. "Nothing," she said. She didn't really feel like getting into her whole theory about how Elizabeth was being so intense about this *Scope* thing because she wanted to avoid thinking about Conner. *I mean, who am I to psychoanalyze Liz?* she reasoned. *Maybe I should just take her at her word. Maybe she does just want to be the next famous news-paper person, like . . . well, like . . . whoever.* "You know, she's been working so hard, maybe she *did* go home sick this time." Jessica looked anxiously at her watch again. "Maybe I should call and check."

"Forget it," Tia said, pushing her thick hair back from her shoulders. "You know she's in the library, Jess."

Jessica glanced at the door again, then back at Tia. "You're right." She took her books from her backpack and piled them on her desk. "All I know is that this madness has got to stop—she has to come out with us tomorrow night, for the sake of her own mental health. Remember, make sure to act all huffy when she gets here. We've got to guilt her hard for missing the pep rally; otherwise she'll never come with us."

"Shhh," Tia said as she looked quickly away from the classroom door.

Elizabeth rushed into class, out of breath, just as the bell rang. "Whew," she said, looking over at Tia. "Barely made it. But I just saw Ms. Dalton way down by the library. It'll probably take her a minute to get here." Elizabeth grinned at her sister and gave her a little wave. "Hey, there," she said. "Haven't seen you in a while."

Jessica murmured a hello and turned in her seat so that she was facing the front of the classroom.

One . . . two . . .

"What's wrong?" Elizabeth asked Jessica.

It's working already, Jessica thought, *and I didn't even get to three.*

Elizabeth turned to Tia, whose eyes were also suddenly glued to the blackboard.

106

"What's the matter, you guys?" Jessica could feel Elizabeth staring at her for several seconds. "Oh, no," she said suddenly. "The pep rally. You're mad because I didn't make it, aren't you?"

Jessica took the cap off her pen and nonchalantly scribbled on her notebook. This was working so well.

"Look, I'm really sorry, Jess," Elizabeth apologized. "I got hung up at work. I heard all about it, though. Everyone says you guys were amazing. You understand, don't you?"

Jessica shrugged and tossed her hair over her shoulder. "No problem," she said, carefully inspecting the doodle she'd just drawn like it was *way* more interesting than Elizabeth's feeble excuses.

Elizabeth turned toward Tia now. "Come on, Tee. Tell her I didn't mean it."

But Tia, just as Jessica hoped, gave her a cool smile and said, "No problemo, Liz. Don't worry about it."

Jessica fought to keep the smile off her face as Elizabeth sighed and slouched in her chair. "Well, I said I was sorry, and I am," she said. "I feel really bad, okay?"

All right, enough. Time to move in for the kill. "Okay, then," Jessica said, turning to look at her at last. "If you feel that bad, I guess we can forgive you."

"I do, Jess." Elizabeth's eyes were full of concern and

also what looked like a bit of confusion. "I just . . . I guess I just didn't know it meant all that much to you."

Jessica shrugged. "It did."

"I'm sorry," Elizabeth repeated. "How can I make it up to you?"

Jessica caught Tia's eye for a second, and the two of them exchanged smiles. "Well," she said, "now that you mention it, there is this one thing."

"What?" Elizabeth leaned forward in her chair eagerly. "Anything. Just tell me and I'll do it, I swear."

Jessica cleared her throat. "The four of us are going out tomorrow night. Me, Tia, Trent, and Jeremy. Why don't you come with us?"

"Oh," Elizabeth said, her face falling a little.

Jessica knew why. If there was anything Elizabeth hated, it was playing third wheel. Or in this case, fifth wheel. She decided to lay it on a little thicker. "We thought being out with us for the whole evening would give you a chance to get to know Trent better and to actually see how great he and Tia are together," she said, nodding to Tia. "But of course, if you don't want to . . ."

"No, no," Elizabeth protested, "it isn't that."

"What is it, then?" Tia asked. Her voice was kind of sharp. "Liz, Trent is so awesome. I just know the two of you will really like each other. And he was really looking forward to meeting you last night—"

Okay, now they had her. Jessica watched as Elizabeth stared down at her desk for what seemed like forever. Finally she said, "Well, I guess I do owe you guys."

"So is that a yes?" Jessica asked.

"Okay," Elizabeth said.

"Great." Jessica had to stop herself from pumping her fist in the air and shouting, "Yes! Victory!" Instead she just said, "We're going to the Zephyr Grille. Be there at seven, okay?"

"Yeah, okay," Elizabeth said, just as Ms. Dalton came into the classroom. "And you know, I really am sorry."

"Oh, it's okay," Jessica replied, really meaning it this time. Again she exchanged a knowing smile with Tia. "Believe me, this will more than make up for it."

Late that night Elizabeth sat at her desk, her computer monitor glowing in front of her, looking much too blank and gray. She took a moment to stretch, then glanced at the alarm clock by her bed again and groaned. Already past midnight. She was up way too late, but she just couldn't even think about sleeping until she got this proposal written. And she couldn't get the proposal written because she couldn't figure out how to write it without naming Ken.

Elizabeth placed her hands deliberately on the keyboard again and furiously typed an all-caps headline across the page: HIGH-SCHOOL RE-CRUITS GONE HAYWIRE? Underneath she wrote, "Everyone loves a football star. And when the star is a local high-school player who gets offered a major college scholarship, the whole town rallies behind him...."

Elizabeth stopped to read what she'd written, then triple clicked the sentence and deleted it, just like she'd deleted every opening she'd written so far. How could she even mention anything about a local player who was offered a major scholarship? Gee, think anyone might trace that back to Ken?

She sat up again and shook her head furiously. Okay, she had to snap out of it. She'd just try a different approach.

SCHOLARSHIP FRAUD, she typed. Underneath it she began, *Have you ever wondered just how high-school athletic scholarships are decided? Are they based solely on a player's merit and his or her potential worth to the team? Are they always given to the best and the brightest? Well, sometimes it seems these aren't always the criteria for choosing scholarship recipients....*

She paused for a minute to reread what she'd written. Ugh! If she'd come across this first paragraph in a magazine article, she'd have turned the page long ago. She pushed her mouse away and pressed her hands against her eyes. "It's boring,"

Elizabeth said aloud. "Joanna's never going to want to read this—even I don't want to read it, and I wrote it!"

Again she selected the text and hit the delete key. She threw her head back against her chair and stared at the ceiling. Why couldn't she just say what she wanted to say? It was like there was something holding her back. . . .

Elizabeth combed her fingers through her hair, thinking despite herself about how long and thick it suddenly felt. Probably time for another cut. Hmmm. Maybe she'd even have it styled this time. Treat herself. It was all about her now, after all.

Suddenly she sat up straight in her chair and stared at the monitor again. *Wait a minute,* she thought, *that's right! I'm doing it again! I've been getting too wrapped up in how everyone will react to this thing, and I don't even know if it's going to be published yet. No wonder I can't write it.*

Okay, she was just going to get it all down. That's all—she'd just write it out. Then she'd go back and take out all the specific details.

Quickly Elizabeth began to type out her thoughts—her own personal perceptions and feelings about what Maria had told her. There was nothing wrong with that, right? After all, she was just writing about herself.

It's been a long road for a friend I know, she wrote. *A star high-school quarterback who thought his sought-after scholarship to a major university was the result of diligence and skill. But now this person knows differently. . . ."*

Again, thoughts of even these lines leading back to Ken started to nudge into her brain. But Elizabeth closed her eyes and said out loud, "I'm just writing out the facts. I'll go back later and edit everything, delete names, whatever."

For some reason, this seemed to clear her head, and Elizabeth was finally able to dig in and start writing her proposal for real. Before she knew it, she was in total "journalism mode," and her fingers were flying across the keys. She had to admit, it felt good. Like she was in control at last.

I can do this, she realized as she read over what she'd written. She was definitely going to publish something in that magazine, and nothing was going to stop her.

Not even a nagging feeling in her gut and a conscience ready to explode.

Jessica Wakefield

To: trent#1@cal.rr.com
From: jess1@cal.rr.com
Subject: Fix up

Hey, Trent! Liz is definitely on for tomorrow night! So grab one of your buddies—make sure he's a hottie, by the way—and let's get this little party started. Oh, and feel free to tell whoever you pick what we're planning here. The only one who needs to be surprised is the victim herself.

—Jess

PS: Let me know who you come up with!

Trent Maynor

To: jess1@cal.rr.com
From: trent#1@cal.rr.com
Subject: re: Fix up

Jess, I've already told a couple of potentials around here that I wanted to set up your identical twin—and let's just say that the word has gotten out. Guys I've never even seen before are coming up to me in the hallway! Now my only problem is going to be picking the best one.

I'm going to see if any of these guys are willing to wash my car in exchange for the date . . . or maybe give me some money.

Just kidding! :-)

—Trent

CHAPTER
Righteous Indignation

8

Ken burst through the front door of his house and headed straight for the kitchen, where he knew his letter of intent was lying on the table, untouched since he'd stared at it over breakfast this morning. Today was Friday, his last day to sign with Michigan. The moment of truth had arrived.

He'd decided. All week long he'd been leaning toward saying *no*. The way his dad had acted at the dinner with Coach Garrett—telling Ken how to think, how to feel—it had made him sick. But then Ken had passed Will on his way to the SVH parking lot this afternoon. Will didn't say anything, he just gave Ken a thumbs-up sign. And that was when Ken had really made up his mind.

He was going to Michigan. He would be stupid to throw away this opportunity just to spite his dad. If Ken didn't take the scholarship, it would just go to somebody else with connections. The school was good, the team was good, the coach was good . . . what more did he want? All he had to do was sign the letter and call Coach Garrett, and the deal would be done. Nobody ever had to know. These things happened all the time.

Ken picked up a pen from the little cup by the phone and sat down at the table. Before he had a chance to second-guess himself (*Second-guess?—try five-hundredth guess*), he scribbled his full name at the bottom and printed the date beside it.

There. Done. And immediately a rush of relief flooded through him. Not relief that he had finally made the right decision—because he wasn't sure he had—relief that he had simply made *a* decision. *The* decision. It was enough to make him want to scream or shout or tear around the block a few times like a little kid. Thank God it was over.

Now he leafed through the papers and college catalogs that Coach Garrett had given him, all of them stacked in a pile on the table beside him, until he found the coach's business card. Ken picked up the phone and dialed the number, anxious to hear the coach's voice welcoming him aboard. But after several rings a young guy's voice answered instead.

"Coach Garrett's office," the voice said, "Adam Stewart speaking."

"Oh, uh, hi," Ken said. "I'd like to speak to Coach Garrett, please."

"Sorry, he's not here right now. I'm the assistant trainer. Can I help you with anything?"

Ordinarily Ken would have simply said no, thanks and called back later. But he was feeling so great from having made his decision that he was suddenly eager to hear all about Michigan's football program. What was the harm in talking to the guy for a minute? After all, they'd be working together next year.

"My name is Ken Matthews and—"

"Ken Matthews?" Ken heard the sound of papers shuffling. "We've been recruiting you, haven't we?"

Ken smiled at the receiver. "That's right." *Wow, they already know me. They really do treat their players well. . . .* "Anyway, since I've got you on the phone, maybe I can get your honest opinion on something," Ken went on. "What's it like working for the coach? He seems like he really knows how to run a team."

"Oh, he's great," Adam said. "He knows everything about football, and he gets the most out of everyone. He keeps this place hopping. But in a good way."

Ken began to smile, feeling even better now. Obviously his instincts were right on this one. Garrett was a good guy—just the kind of coach he'd want to play for.

"Yeah," Adam continued, "we're all just sick about this deal he's signing. We're definitely going to miss him around here."

117

Ken froze. *Wait—did I just hear him right?* Ken opened his mouth, but when he tried to speak, his tongue wouldn't work right. Finally he forced the words out. "What do you mean?" he asked thickly.

"He's going to the NFL next year. I'm surprised you hadn't heard—it's been in all of the papers up here." Adam sighed. "Yeah, for a while we thought he'd stick around, but it's pretty much a done deal by now. They just have to work out the details—you know, salary and benefits and guarantees and all. If you ask me, he needs to be pretty careful with the guarantees because that's where they can screw you. I heard about this one guy . . ."

"Thanks," Ken said, letting the phone drop from his hand and back onto the cradle.

Feeling completely numb, he stood up, then sat back down. He picked up the pen, then set it right back where it was. His heart seemed to be trying to jump out of his chest, and he nearly had to struggle to breathe. How could they have sat through that dinner and not told him? Coach Garrett had told him how the team would be run—told him he wouldn't have to be redshirted—when he knew he wouldn't even be around to make sure it happened. So what if the coach didn't know about the bribe? That didn't make him honest. The one person he'd finally trusted in this whole mess had

118

turned out to be as full of crap as the rest of them!

Ken stared at the pile of papers and books on the table in front of him. He couldn't believe how much time he'd spent looking at all of that stuff—worrying over every detail while it had slowly eaten him up. The anger welled up inside him until he thought he would burst.

In one sudden move he swept his arm across the table and heaved all of it off the edge. Books and papers slammed into the far wall, then crashed onto the floor in a giant heap.

Ken stared down at the mess, reminding himself to breathe. He had to try to calm down. Otherwise he thought he might just totally lose it. He took a few deep breaths, then finally bent down and started sorting through the papers again. After a minute he found his letter of intent. He stood up, staring at the blur of words on the page, thinking of how long he'd waited to hold a thing like this in his hands, of how much he'd always loved football. And how, in the end, none of it had meant a thing to anyone but him.

He grasped the top of the letter in both hands and slowly ripped it from top to bottom, then placed those pieces together and tore it again and again until he had shredded it into a hundred tiny scraps.

He tossed the flecks of paper into the air and watched them float softly down onto the shiny kitchen linoleum. For a crazy instant he thought of how it almost looked like confetti. How it *should* have been confetti. If only he'd never picked up that phone.

If only he still had something to celebrate.

As she rushed from the elevator into the *Scope's* newsroom that afternoon, Elizabeth sped through the lobby, barely remembering to say a quick hello to Dora. She wanted to get straight to Joanna Perry's office and give her the proposal before anything could distract her. She strode briskly down the hallway, sliding the document out of her bag as she went. The thickness of it surprised her—she'd only meant to write a one-page summary. But it had somehow wound up being three pages, even after she'd gone back and edited out as many details as possible. Now she'd just have to hand it off and see what happened.

As she was turning the corner that led to Joanna's office, Leo Grant appeared at the far end of the hallway. "Elizabeth! Thank God you're here!" he cried, immediately rushing over and touching her elbow. Elizabeth tried to ignore the tingling she felt there. "I've got to get some quick research done on a piece before deadline. Think you can handle it?" His deep brown eyes gazed into hers, and Elizabeth felt her heart thump with excitement—excitement over the opportunity to do some important work for a change, of course.

"Oh! Sure, I can handle it," she promised. "I just need to talk to Joanna for one sec—"

"This is really urgent, Liz. Anyway, Joanna's on deadline too." Leo motioned to Joanna's office. "Whenever her door's closed like that, it means she doesn't want to be interrupted."

Before Elizabeth knew what was happening, Leo had steered her over to an empty desk, placed her in front of a computer, and given her a list of Web sites to check for information on some new sanitation law the city council was proposing. Elizabeth quickly laid down her bag, giving only a fleeting thought to her proposal before grabbing the mouse and jumping into cyberspace.

It was interesting work. The more Elizabeth read, the more she realized how big an impact the law would have on Sweet Valley, and she soon found herself caught up in the particulars of the story. She spent the rest of the afternoon and then the first part of the evening checking and rechecking the facts from the article and clearing the new information with Leo. By the time she was finished, she had a stiff neck but also a slew of good statistics.

"This is great stuff," Leo said to her when Elizabeth handed it all over at last. "Great work." Elizabeth glowed with the compliment. "Thanks, Elizabeth!" he called over his shoulder as he rushed off to the production area.

Elizabeth smiled, positively charged with excitement. So this was what it was like to work under tight deadlines. No wonder people got such a rush out of journalism. She looked around the newsroom with a real sense of satisfaction, feeling like an actual member of the team now.

Wait a minute, she realized all at once, *what team?* The room was nearly cleared out—only a couple of people wandered between the cubicles or sat typing at their desks. *Oh God—what time is it?* Elizabeth checked the clock above the entrance. Ten after seven! She was late for Jessica's dinner!

Oh, no. Her sister was going to *kill* her. And she still had to give her proposal to Joanna! She grabbed her things and sprinted down the hallway. But when she reached Joanna's office, she saw that it was dark and her computer was turned off. Her heart sank.

"She took the rest of her work home," a deep voice behind her said. Elizabeth turned to see Leo standing there, another folder in his hand.

Elizabeth let out a small sigh. "Oh, well. It can wait until Monday, I guess." She turned to leave and gave Leo a small wave. "Have a good weekend."

"Actually," Leo said, "I was hoping you weren't going just yet."

"Oh. Well," Elizabeth hedged, "I kind of have to be somewhere." She checked her watch again. Seven-fifteen. "Actually, I'm pretty late."

"That's really too bad." Leo looked practically de-flated. "I have this other article that needs to run in this issue. It's a criminal investigation on a case of identity theft. Lost credit cards? Maybe you've heard something about it already—"

"Yeah!" Elizabeth said. "All those people got ripped off—it was in all the papers."

"Well, the papers don't know half the story," Leo said, his eyes twinkling with excitement. "We just found out some new information. At first everyone assumed it was one person acting alone—but we've got some proof that it was a *conspiracy*. We were going to hold it for the next issue, but we want to scoop everyone else. I was hoping, since you wanted some real reporting experience, maybe you'd want to call some of these sources and check the facts with them? Even get a few quotes for us."

Elizabeth nearly dropped her things. *Quotes? Like a real reporter? Is he kidding?* "Oh, of course I could!" she said. Finally! She was going to get some real hard-core experience here—thank God she was working with Leo. He really understood what it was like to be trying to get your foot in the door. "I just have to make one quick call."

Pushing away the guilty thoughts that were edg-ing in on her brain, Elizabeth grabbed a phone book from a stack on one of the desks and dialed the

Zephyr Grille. Elizabeth left a brief message for Jessica and hung up. Jessica would just *have* to understand. This was Elizabeth's big chance, and she couldn't turn it down.

She picked the phone back up and dialed the first source on Leo's list.

Thank God for Maria, Ken thought as he pulled into her driveway. Luckily they already had a date planned for tonight, even though it wasn't supposed to be for another couple of hours. But he hadn't known what to do with himself. He'd sat staring at the pile of papers on the kitchen floor for what seemed like an hour before he'd finally gotten up and gone to his car, leaving the kitchen a wreck.

He'd felt this great surge of energy when he'd left the house. But in the ten minutes it took to drive to Maria's, he'd found the time to beat himself up instead for what he'd just done. If he'd made a mistake, it was a huge one. The biggest one of his life.

Now all he could think of was seeing Maria's face and holding her. He just wanted her to tell him that he'd done the right thing and that everything would be okay.

But when she opened the door, the look on her face didn't exactly fill him with warm, fuzzy feelings. "What are you doing here?" she demanded.

Ken stood there, gaping at her. He was so surprised

by her anger, he simply couldn't make his mouth form any words. Thankfully, he didn't need to. After one close look at the state he was in, Maria's face suddenly softened, and she took his hand. "Ken, what's wrong?" she asked. She stepped out onto the porch with him and closed the door behind her.

He shook his head and looked down at the painted wood floor of the porch. But Maria took his face in her hands and gently forced him to look up at her. "What *is* it?" she said. "Tell me."

He struggled for a minute, and then a choked sound came out of his throat. "It's over," he finally managed to say. "I'm not going."

And suddenly Maria's arms were around him, just like he'd hoped, and she was squeezing him so tight, he couldn't move. "It's okay," she said, her breath warm against his ear. After a minute she pulled away from him and led him over to the front steps, where they always sat and talked, looking out onto the tree-lined sidewalk in front of her house. As he sat down beside her, she took both of his hands in hers. "Tell me everything," she said.

He squeezed her fingers tightly. "Well, I *was* going. I mean, I'd decided, Maria. I came home today and grabbed the letter and signed it, and then I called to tell Coach Garrett, but he wasn't there. I got this other guy instead—an assistant trainer or something. He started talking about what a great guy the coach was and how they were all going to miss him next year."

Her forehead creased with confusion. "What does that mean?" she asked.

"That's what I wanted to know," Ken said through clenched teeth. "He's signed on with a pro team for next year." He took his hands away from her and ran them through his hair. "It's all been one big lie, Maria. Starting with the day I thought I got this scholarship fair and square." He couldn't even look at her now, couldn't stand turning around and seeing what he knew would be pity in her eyes. "Anyway, I guess I'd better go," Ken croaked. "It looks like I caught you in the middle of something. I'll come back later—"

Maria grabbed his arm. "Ken, don't you dare leave. I was just studying. I can do that anytime." He looked into her eyes and was relieved to see that there wasn't any trace of pity there, only a fiery glint of anger. "Let me ask you a question," she said.

Ken nodded. "Okay."

"Would you change anything now if you could? Take it back? Still go to Michigan?"

Her dark eyes locked onto his, demanding an answer. He didn't even have to think. "No," he said, realizing it was one of the easiest questions he'd ever answered. Of course he wouldn't. All the arguments in his head—he had to work to think of the arguments in favor of going. But the reasons for not going were so present, so obvious, he didn't even really need to think about them at all.

"I know." Maria squeezed his hand. "I've known for a long time, and I knew you'd figure it out too."

For an instant he couldn't find his tongue. "But . . . you never said . . ."

"What was I supposed to do—tell you your own mind?" Maria's smile faded now. She reached down and picked up a pebble from the steps. "I knew what you were going through, Ken, but I never told you how I felt about it. I thought you needed to decide for yourself." She shook her head and threw the pebble onto the ground. "I never wanted you to take that scholarship. Even though you really *do* deserve it. Whether you believe that or not."

Ken let go a breath he hadn't realized he'd been holding. He reached down and took her hand again. "I couldn't have gotten through this without you, Maria. Anyway, you're the one who told me from the start to go with my instincts, and my instincts were screaming at me not to go. If I'd listened to you, I wouldn't have wasted so much time on this whole fiasco. My time *and* yours." Suddenly he remembered something he'd been meaning to ask her about. "Maria, what was Melissa talking about the other day?"

Maria looked away. "What do you mean?"

Ken folded his arms across his chest. "She mentioned something about your grades—" he prompted.

Maria sighed. "Yeah. They haven't been the greatest lately. That's why I was studying when you drove up. I've got a major French test on Monday, and if I don't ace it, my average is going into the toilet." She looked up at him and smiled weakly. "I guess I've just had my mind on other things lately...."

"Like on me." Ken shook his head. *I can't believe I've spent so much mental energy on this that I didn't even notice Maria was having trouble,* he thought. *How did I get so wrapped up in myself?*

"Don't blame yourself. I *wanted* to help you." Ken looked at her, and in an instant Maria's arms were behind his neck, and she drew him into one of the hottest, longest kisses he could remember. When she finally pulled away from him, her eyes were dancing over his. "And now let's celebrate," she said firmly. "How about an early dinner, then some late night dancing at the Riot?" She threw up her arms and gave a little dance move.

Ken laughed, then drew her into him again, wrapping his arms around her. "How about," he said, "just dinner, then straight back here, so I can help you study?"

Maria grinned. "Wild man," she teased. "You sure know how to show a girl a good time."

Ken held her tightly, feeling a warm breeze wash over them. It was funny, he thought, the way life could be. One minute it was the end of the world. And the next minute it was . . . well . . . *Maria.*

Alanna Feldman

Okay, he's definitely avoiding me. Even I can figure that out. Conner's not the kind of guy to get so wrapped up in schoolwork, he can't dial a phone. I keep thinking about the last time we were together. Could he tell that I was practically wasted? I know I'm an expert at covering it up. I own the strongest mouthwashes they make. But maybe he smelled it on me anyway. After all, he's an expert too.

Oh God. I think I've screwed up big this time.

Conner McDermott

I can't keep avoiding her. Not just because it's making me feel like a jerk to blow her off this way, but because as usual, I can't stop thinking about her. Sooner or later I'm going to have to level with her, and then things could get rough.

Alanna has to stop drinking. I can't have it any other way. But I know she's the only one who can make that decision, and unless she does . . .

Well, yeah. And that's exactly why I've been avoiding her.

That Disaster-Prone Element

Jessica traced her finger over her paper place mat and eyed the restaurant doors again. Elizabeth was late, and she felt like she needed to reassure Trent, Tia, and Jeremy, and especially C. J., the guy Trent had brought for Elizabeth, that her sister would definitely be here. But the longer they all waited, the more tense things got. And Tia certainly wasn't helping, pointing secretively at her watch every time she caught Jessica's eye.

"Hey, C. J.," Jessica said, "Trent says you're a writer." Inwardly she cringed at her slip. This was the topic she'd been saving for when Elizabeth arrived. She'd planned to play up their mutual interests right from the start.

"Well, I'm on the annual staff. And I write for the school paper and all," he said, shrugging. C. J. had light brown hair and beautiful pale blue eyes. He wasn't particularly buff, but he wasn't skinny either. Almost built like Conner, Jessica thought, which was probably a good thing. Trent had excelled, as far as she was concerned. This guy was definitely Elizabeth's type. If only she'd show up to meet him!

Before she could ask another question, a waiter began to make his way toward the table. "Oh, good," Jessica said. "I need a giant Coke or something." But instead of taking their drink orders, the waiter stopped in front of their table and unfolded a slip of paper. "Jessica Wakefield?" he asked, looking from Jessica to Tia.

"That's me," Jessica said, startled.

"I have a message for you," he said. "It's from a Liz Wakefield?"

Jessica gulped. *Oh, no, oh, no, oh, no.*

"She said to tell you she has to work late and she's very, very sorry, but she won't be able to make it tonight."

"*What?*" Jessica cried.

"Oh, no," Tia said, leaning her forehead into her hand. "I knew this would be a disaster."

"Tia!" Jessica whispered, then glanced over at poor C. J., who looked like he wanted to crawl under the table.

The waiter stood uncomfortably for a moment, then gave Jessica an apologetic look. "She did ask me to be sure to say, 'Very, very sorry.' If that helps."

"Thanks," Jessica said miserably, and the guy quickly disappeared.

Jessica glanced over at C. J., finding it hard to actually look at him. "I'm so incredibly sorry," she said. "I don't know what is going on with her, really. I just . . . I had no idea. . . ."

"It's okay," he said. He shook his head and laughed. "It happens. I should have known. My luck is never this good."

Cute *and* sweet. *Elizabeth has no idea what she's missing.*

Jessica looked over at Jeremy, who said nothing. He was just shaking his head at Jessica, with a didn't-I-tell-you-so? expression on his face. Somehow it was enough to make Jessica feel like the most naive, gullible, incredibly stupid person on the—

"Hey," Trent said. "Don't feel bad, Jess. You were just trying to do something nice." He gave her a smile that instantly made her feel better.

"Thanks, Trent." Jessica flashed him a smile, then glanced back at her boyfriend to see if he would agree.

Jeremy stared down at the table, a dark look on his face.

"Look, it's not your fault, Jess," said Tia, "but this was kind of a disaster waiting to happen, don't you think? No offense to you, C. J."

"No," C. J. said, "you're right. Fix ups always kind of have that disaster-prone element."

"I just can't believe it," Jessica said, trying to be

careful not to bad-mouth her sister in front of the others. But she was so furious, she couldn't help herself. "I mean, don't those places close on Friday nights, like the rest of the world?"

C. J. smiled at her. "Oh, no way," he said. "My mom edits a weekly newsletter. She's spent lots of Friday nights on deadline. She comes home after midnight sometimes, after making a FedEx run to the airport. It's just the business."

"I guess," Jessica admitted, sighing. "But I'm talking about my *sister*. Doesn't family mean anything?"

"Hey," C. J. protested, "I'm talking about my *mom!*"

Everyone cracked up at that, and Jessica felt a little more relaxed. Finally Jeremy put his arm around her shoulders. "It's okay, Jess," he said. "Liz would have come if she could. Why don't we all just forget about it and figure out what we're eating?" He picked up his menu in front of Jessica so they could both look at it.

The five of them glanced over their menus for a moment. Then Trent's eyes appeared over the top of his. "I know how you feel, Jess," he whispered. "I think family comes first too."

She smiled at him again and mouthed, "Thank you." It was nice to know that *somebody* got it.

*　　*　　*

135

No matter how many basketball games she'd played, the thing that always struck Jade was the sound of ten pairs of squeaking rubber soles cutting and turning on the slick gym floor. The constant little peeps and squeals of the shoes gave her such a charge—like everything around her was happening in excited little bursts of energy.

Now the sound seemed to be revving her up for the game ahead as she stood in line for her turn during the layup drill just before the game. She breathed the hot, stale air of the gym, watching her teammates fly at the goal one by one. They were paired off in two lines, and after each shot the person from the other line grabbed the rebound and passed it to the next girl in the shooting line. Then the shooter ran to the end of the rebound line and started again.

Soon it was Jade's turn. She ran forward, dribbled twice, made a smooth, easy layup, then continued toward the end of the line. But when she rounded the corner, she nearly stopped in her tracks.

Evan.

At the sight of his face this strange, tingling feeling hit her, like she was about to be struck by lightning. She had to fight to compose herself long enough to keep running and take her place in line, all the while turning her head so she wouldn't lose sight of him. What was he doing here? Had he come to see her? But he didn't even seem to be looking her way. Should she wave or let him know she saw him? Jade stared at him intently, but it was hard to tell if he was staring back since he was so far on the other side of the gym.

Wait a minute. What's he doing on the other side of the gym—the Big Mesa side?

She didn't have time to think about it. It was her turn to rebound now.

By the time Coach Warner called them in from the warm-up drill, Jade had broken a sweat. She sprinted to the bench and sat down, wiping her face with a towel. The coach began giving them instructions, running down their basic strategy for the game, but Jade was having a hard time paying attention to what she was saying. She couldn't stop glancing toward Evan.

After a few minutes the coach took Andrea Stevens aside to talk with her about her specific assignment, and Jade let her mind wander again, still wondering why Evan was sitting across the gym. *Maybe he's confused. Or maybe he's feeling too weird about what happened at HOJ to come any closer. Maybe . . .*

"—because Evan Plummer is no basketball fan, that's for sure," Jade heard someone say.

What? She whipped her head around to see

Denise Yates and Tammy Blankenship, two girls who used to go to El Carro, sitting on the bench next to her. They were leaning toward each other with their heads down, speaking in hushed voices and nodding toward Evan as they talked. "Well, he's obviously into her, then," Denise said. "Why else would he be here?"

He's into her? Are they talking about me? But why wouldn't they just tell me straight out—or be quieter, at least? Don't they know I'm sitting right here?

Tammy smiled and twisted the band around her sleek, blond ponytail to tighten it. "Well, all I can say is, good for her. It's about time Roni found someone decent."

Jade felt like someone had thrown a basketball straight into her stomach. *Roni? Oh God. He's here to see that airhead?*

Just as the knowledge of this sank in, Jade saw Roni moving across the gym toward Evan. She waved as she passed him—very enthusiastically, it seemed—and grinned when he waved back.

What's wrong with me? I can't believe I'm just now figuring this out! Obviously Evan's moved on. I guess that's why he wanted me to meet him and his "friend" at HOJ. So I'd get the message.

Jade turned away, tearing her eyes away from Evan. She gazed down at the floor instead, at the dull reflection of lights along the polished surface. A tear splashed down on her sneaker, and she leaned over, pretending to be tying her shoelace. She let her hair fall over her face. Jade took a few deep breaths and tried to gain control of herself.

There was no way she was going to let the other team's star forward see her cry.

By nine o'clock Elizabeth was finally wrapping things up at the office. She was exhausted but still really pumped, knowing how great a job she'd done tonight. Leo had complimented her again on the way she'd handled the source checking, and she'd gotten some excellent quotes out of the people she called. "You're a natural, Liz," Leo had said. "This is definitely the right line of work for you. If you like it, that is."

Like it? I love it, Elizabeth thought. She'd especially loved how electric the whole place got as the deadline drew closer. Even though there were only a few people left at the office—the quiet air seemed to crackle with energy. Elizabeth realized that her whole life, she'd been so organized, she'd hardly ever had to rush to finish anything. But in a weird way— the rush *was* a rush. No wonder some people said they worked best under pressure.

After powering down the computer she'd been using, Elizabeth reached under the desk for her bag and saw her proposal sticking out of the top. She sighed, thinking about how long she would have to wait until she saw Joanna again—not until Monday. It killed her to think she'd stayed up so late last night to finish it and now no one would see it for days. Shaking her head, she picked up her bag and began to walk toward the door. *Oh, well, at least I'll have the weekend to make sure the proposal is really tight.* Then she noticed Leo across the room, gathering his things to leave too.

Wait a minute. I could just give this to Leo, Elizabeth realized. *After all, he is my supervisor. He could read it over the weekend. If he thinks it's good, he could pass it on to Joanna for me, and if he thinks it needs some work, maybe he could give me a few pointers.*

Elizabeth smiled to herself, thinking that it wouldn't be so painful to have a few extra reasons to chat with adorable Leo. Pulling the proposal out of her bag, she walked toward him. He was sitting with his head down, his back toward Elizabeth, as he piled things into a dark green backpack. But just as she reached his desk, the phone rang. Elizabeth stopped and waited to see if the call would be a short one.

"*Scope,*" Leo said into the receiver, "Leo speaking . . . oh, hey, Joanna, how's the article coming?"

Elizabeth stifled a groan. He'd definitely be on the phone for a while if he was talking to Joanna. *I'll just go home,* she decided. *Maybe I'll ask for Leo's advice on Monday.* Elizabeth had just turned to walk away when she heard Leo say, "Yeah. Things went just great tonight—once I got all those sources checked, anyway."

Elizabeth stopped in her tracks, then wheeled around. Leo still had his back to her. Obviously he didn't have clue one about the fact that she was standing there. Elizabeth stood perfectly still, hardly breathing, wondering if she could have possibly heard him right.

"You won't believe the quote I got out of Chief Brandon," Leo said, laughing. "You know how he hardly ever does more than grunt? I don't know why, but he was chatting up a storm tonight. I've got him going on and on about how out of hand local crime is these days."

Elizabeth's mouth dropped open. That was *her* quote! It had taken her almost twenty minutes of prodding to get the chief to say that. What did Leo think he was doing?

"No problem," Leo said. "You're totally welcome. Right. See you Monday."

Elizabeth stood frozen as Leo hung up the phone, then got up from his chair and turned around. Elizabeth hoped the glare she was giving him would be enough to knock him back into a sitting position, but Leo merely smiled and said, "Hey, Liz. I thought you'd gone already."

Elizabeth's heart was thumping in her chest. For a minute she wished her twin was there. Jessica was really good at confrontations, whereas Elizabeth totally dreaded them. Still, she wasn't about to leave without calling Leo on taking credit for *her* work. Her palms suddenly turned sweaty, but she fought back her nervousness and forced herself to speak.

"Well, I'm still here," Elizabeth said. "And I heard what you told Joanna." She folded her arms across her chest.

Leo didn't even flinch. The small smile still played on his lips as he said, "Oh, you did." He picked up a folder from the desk and leafed through it. "Well, let's see. How can I explain this. . . ."

He isn't even going to apologize? Elizabeth couldn't believe it. Just a few minutes ago she'd actually thought this guy was cute—thought he was going to help her with her career as a journalist. But now he was acting like a total sleaze! "Yes, how *can* you explain taking credit for my work?" she demanded. A lump rose in her throat, but she forced it down. *Be professional,* she told herself. Elizabeth took a deep breath. "I think that was really unfair of you, Leo," she said calmly.

Leo sighed, then stepped out from behind his

desk and stood to face Elizabeth. He looked her in the eye and said, "Look, it's nothing personal. I already told you what a great job you did tonight. You *got* credit, Liz. From *me*."

"But—"

"You just don't understand the nature of the business yet," he went on smoothly. "I can't tell you how many times this same thing happened to me when I was interning. I worked my butt off for my supervisors, and they never said a word to management either." He shrugged. "I'm sorry, Liz. It's just the way of the peon."

Elizabeth stared at him, dumbstruck. She had absolutely no idea how to respond. Clearly Leo didn't feel an ounce of guilt over what he'd done. He didn't think of it as a betrayal at all. *What can I say that's going to change his mind?* she wondered. But she knew the answer—nothing at all. Finally she turned and left without saying another word.

As soon as she pushed open the door, the cool evening air rushed over her, and she stopped to breathe it in for a moment, hoping to calm her nerves. Above the trees in the parking lot sat a low orange moon and a sky speckled with stars. It was all perfectly peaceful and serene. But Elizabeth's anger swelled inside her until the tears she'd been holding back finally stung her eyes. This dream job

143

was turning into a nightmare. She could stand the long hours and intense work—but she couldn't stand dishonest people. How could Leo be such a backstabber? How could Elizabeth not have seen it coming? And how was she ever going to make it in such a cutthroat business?

Jade Wu

Okay, no more thinking about Evan. I've got a game going here, and it's time to focus on strategy. This isn't personal or anything. It's just business. I'm going to crush Roni Johnson—I mean, the Big Mesa team. She—I mean <u>they</u>—are going to be sorry they ever showed up tonight.

And I don't care who's here to watch.

CHAPTER
Personal Gain
10

Watching Roni at the start of the game on Friday night, Evan decided she was a good offensive player, but she put up too many shots on her own. She definitely needed to pass more when her teammates were open and let them score once in a while. He made a mental note to tell her this, like he'd said he would. Before the game she'd come over and asked him to watch her closely and let her know where she could stand to improve. Evan, of course, was always willing to help out a friend.

Now it was five minutes into the first quarter, and Evan hadn't taken his eyes off her once. But that wasn't just because of his promise to her. He hadn't taken his eyes off Roni because if he did, he knew just who he would look at, and then the whole rest of the game would be a blurry haze—one big backdrop for Jade.

He'd barely had time to make this resolution when Jade stole the ball from a Big Mesa player and sprinted toward the SVH basket, her teammates racing behind her. Evan grinned. Jade looked awesome out there—she was a column of power in white and red as she flew down the court, blue-black ponytail whipping around behind her. At the hoop she leaped up and laid the ball off the backboard, then through the net in one smooth motion. Evan let out a loud whoop before remembering where he was sitting. He looked around sheepishly as a couple of Big Mesa kids glared at him. Evan decided he'd better keep quiet.

The first half flew by, and when it ended, Sweet Valley was up by ten points. Jade had contributed eleven points, including one huge three pointer. Roni had scored a few baskets too, although Evan wasn't really sure how many. As the Big Mesa team headed for the locker room, Roni stopped to talk to Evan. She stood on the bleachers, stretching out her calves as she spoke. "Hey," she said breathlessly. "What do you think of the game?" She flashed a huge smile at him.

"It's great," he said, then caught himself. "I mean—I'm sorry you guys are behind, but the game is pretty exciting."

Roni waved him off. "No problem. I'm just warming up. We'll catch up after halftime—that's when it counts anyway." She straightened one leg and touched her nose to her knee.

147

"Good point," Evan agreed. "Do you want your notes now?"

Roni looked up at him and gave a confused little giggle. "What?"

"I was watching you, like you asked," Evan explained. "I saw a couple of things you can work on in the second half, like I was thinking you might want to pass the ball more. Let your teammates put it up for you. That way, you know, you can keep the other team off balance." He felt a flash of guilt for helping Roni against Jade's team, but he decided that SVH didn't really need his help, and Roni *had* asked for it.

But a second later Evan was sorry he'd said anything at all. A look came over Roni's face that told him she probably wasn't really after constructive criticism after all. "Well," she said, "for someone who doesn't pay much attention to basketball, you sure have a lot to say about it. Anyway, I'm glad you're enjoying the game. I'll see you in the second half." She turned abruptly and trotted after the rest of her teammates as they streamed into the locker room.

Evan watched her go, biting his lip. He felt bad for criticizing Roni's game. Then again, if she hadn't really wanted his critique, why had she asked for it?

Halftime ended, and for another forty minutes Evan watched Jade tear up the court. The Sweet Valley fans went completely nuts every time she got the ball, yelling her name and stomping their feet, shaking the bleachers. But Big Mesa pulled out some serious power in the second half. Even though she hadn't seemed to want to hear it, Roni took Evan's advice, shooting pass after pass to her teammates and grabbing the rebounds when they missed the baskets. By the game's end, with less than a minute to go, Big Mesa had actually pulled ahead of Sweet Valley by two points, and Evan found himself wiping his sweaty palms against his pants.

Time was running down. Jade took a pass near midcourt and drove toward the goal. Just then Roni appeared from out of nowhere, cutting her off. For just a second Evan thought he saw the two of them lock eyes. Then the moment was over as Roni lunged at the ball. Jade wheeled around, using her body to keep it away. A second later Cherie set a pick for Jade, giving her an opening. Jade flashed by Roni and put up a shot just at the last instant, but Roni sprang for the block. She got a finger on the ball, hitting Jade's arm as she went.

The ref's whistle blew while the shot hung in the air, and the ball teetered on the rim for what seemed like forever. Finally it fell in. The SVH fans leaped to their feet, screaming. The score was tied, and Jade had picked up the foul from Roni!

Without thinking, Evan jumped up, cheering

along with the other side, yelling and whistling for Jade. After a minute his voice seemed really loud. He looked around and saw everyone on his side of the stands glaring at him. This time, though, it only made him laugh and yell louder. So what if he was the only one cheering on his side of the gym? If these people knew Jade like he did, they'd be cheering too.

Elizabeth walked into the house to find her parents in the den, cuddled together in the dark, watching some old movie. *The standard Friday-night rental,* she thought. They hadn't heard her come in, and she took a minute to gaze through the doorway at them. In the flickering blue glow of the television they looked perfectly at ease, her mom resting her head on her dad's shoulder. Suddenly Elizabeth felt like crying. What had she been doing all week— driving herself crazy with work for people who didn't even appreciate it? She was overwhelmed by the urge to do something simple. Something like what her parents were doing now, sitting on the couch with the person they loved, holding hands.

But her life hadn't been simple at all lately. In fact, it had been anything but, and she had nobody to blame but herself. Being self-centered wasn't all it was cracked up to be.

Elizabeth decided not to disturb them, but she must have made some noise as she turned to leave because her mom said, "Liz?"

Elizabeth turned back. "Hi, guys."

Her mom lifted her head to look at her while her dad pressed the pause button. "What are you doing home?" Alice Wakefield asked.

Elizabeth stared at her, completely uncomprehending, like her brain's hard drive had crashed. *What does she mean? Wasn't I supposed to have been home from work hours ago?*

"Where's Jessica?" her dad asked, leaning forward now, his brow beginning to crease with worry. "Didn't you two have plans together?"

"Oh," Elizabeth said, suddenly remembering. Her original plans for the evening seemed like a lifetime ago—she'd been so busy thinking about Leo that she'd forgotten about Jessica completely. "I had to work late. Jess is probably still out with Jeremy. I never met up with her."

"Oh, honey." Her mother tilted her head sympathetically. "That's too bad. It sounded like Jess had a big night planned."

Elizabeth didn't respond but stood still, staring down at the bag she was still holding. Again she heard Leo's voice telling her it was the "nature of the business" to treat people like crap. Why on earth had she chosen the internship over her own sister?

"Liz?" her father said. "You okay?"

"Yeah," she said. "I'm fine. It was just a long night."

"Why don't you come over here and sit with us?" her mom asked, patting the space on the couch beside her. "You're so busy lately, we hardly ever see you. Your dad made popcorn." She held up a bowl of buttery popcorn.

"Thanks, but I'm beat." It wasn't really true, but Elizabeth just felt like being alone for a while. She had a lot to think about. "I think I'll just go to bed." She had turned to leave when her mother called her back.

"Honey, wait. Before I forget, Maria called. She sounded like it was urgent."

Elizabeth groaned. *Maria?*

Her mom looked confused. "What's wrong?"

"Oh . . . ," Elizabeth hedged, "nothing." That was another lie. Of course, everything was totally wrong, at least as far as Maria was concerned. Elizabeth bit her lip as she thought about her new me-first attitude and that stupid proposal that right now seemed to be burning a huge hole through her bag.

What have I been doing? she thought harshly. *How on earth can I call Leo a backstabber when I was about to ruin one of my best friendships just to get noticed at a magazine?*

Elizabeth slid her proposal out of her bag and held it in front of her. In the light from the television she could barely make out the stupid headline she'd come up with and then the first few words below it.

In one quick motion she ripped it in half and put it back inside her bag.

Her parents stared at her wordlessly, obviously waiting for an explanation. But Elizabeth didn't even know how to begin to explain—not tonight, at least.

"Good night, you guys," she said, then headed for the stairs.

By the time she got to the top, she suddenly felt truly exhausted. She'd have to call Maria tomorrow—after a good night's sleep. And after she'd figured out what in the world she was going to say to her.

Big Mesa's coach signaled for a time-out, just as Jade had expected. It was standard strategy to try to make the shooter feel the pressure before attempting the potentially game-winning free throw. Personally, she thought it was a brilliant move. Free throws were almost one hundred percent mental, and it was pretty easy to get psyched out once you had the chance to realize that the entire outcome of the game rode on whether or not you made the shot. . . .

Which is why I'm not thinking about that, Jade told herself firmly. *I'm just focused on the ball and how I'm going to make it go through the hoop.*

The referee blew his whistle to end the time-out, and Jade stepped to the foul line. She bounced the ball three times, like she always did, then eyed the goal. *Confidence,* she told herself as she took a deep breath. *You can do this.* She could smell the leather of the ball as she held it to her face. She stood there, frozen, and watched as the ball left her fingers and sailed toward the hoop. . . .

Swish.

All net. *We won!*

The final horn sounded, and the already fever-pitched Sweet Valley crowd jumped to its feet, screaming and cheering. Before she knew what was happening, Jade felt one of her teammates grab her from behind, and then her feet lost touch with the ground as six-foot-tall Kadonna Morgan spun her around in circles. Relief washed over Jade, and her body shook with laughter. As soon as she touched the floor again, she was practically submerged in a sea of arms and hands, all hugging her and clapping her on the back. There was Cherie, her face flushed with exertion and excitement. She let out a whoop, and Jade joined her, laughing and yelling until she could hardly breathe.

But even with all of the commotion, she couldn't stop herself from looking for that one face. . . . Jade scanned the crowd, but she didn't have to look very hard. The Big Mesa fans were already clearing out glumly, and only one person stood on their side of the bleachers, grinning and clapping.

Evan.

She'd heard him cheering for her. But . . . wasn't he here with Roni? Jade hesitated, unsure whether to say hello to him. She didn't want to be humiliated when he left with another girl.

But Jade couldn't force herself to leave either, and she stood awkwardly by the bench as the noise subsided and one by one her teammates drifted toward the locker room, each stopping along the way to thump her on the back and congratulate her. She found herself grinning and nodding to each of them but also leaning around them, again trying to catch sight of Evan. *Is he still there? Still alone?*

And then she spotted him—with Roni. For an instant her heart took a dive into her stomach. They *were* together.

But something didn't seem right. There was an odd look about the way Roni was standing, with both hands on her hips and her face only inches from Evan's. Jade couldn't hear what she was saying, but she got the gist of it. Roni looked seriously ticked off. After a few seconds Roni wheeled away and marched to the visitors' locker room, while Evan stood staring after her, a shocked look on his face.

Interesting. But what did it mean? Finally Jade realized that she was the only member of her team who wasn't in the locker room yet. The coach always liked to give them notes after the game, so she really had to get a move on. She grabbed her towel and stopped at the table where cups of water had been set out for the players. She took one and downed it in a single gulp, and when she set the cup back down, she saw that Evan was standing beside her.

"Oh! Hi!" Jade quickly grabbed her towel and began wiping her face and neck. She knew she was a disgusting, sweaty mess, but Evan didn't seem to notice. He stood staring at her, a big, goofy smile on his face, and then he stepped toward her until they were almost nose to nose.

"You were amazing," he said softly. "Not that I'm surprised." His warm brown eyes seemed to dance beneath his dark hair. As hot as she was, Jade felt a wave of heat spread over her.

"Thanks," she said. "I'm glad you, uh, enjoyed the game." Unconsciously she glanced over at the visitors' side, where he had been sitting. "I was surprised to see you sitting on the other side."

Evan shrugged. "I was pulling for the right team, though."

Jade felt a smile spread slowly across her face. "Yeah," she said. "I could see that."

Evan reached out and took hold of both ends of the towel looped around her neck. Then he started to gently pull it, drawing her closer.

Jade put her hand on his chest to stop him. "I should really go shower," she said.

But in the next instant his arms were around her waist, pulling her easily against him. "Sorry," Evan whispered, "I just can't wait that long."

And then his lips were on hers in a kiss that was sweet and somehow familiar, like the first sip of lemonade at the beginning of a long, hot summer season.

And all she could think was, *Neither can I.*

Elizabeth Wakefield

Things to do tomorrow:

1. Apologize to Jessica for blowing her off so much lately.
2. Apologize to Maria for not being there for her more.
3. Decide if I'm keeping this internship.
4. Figure out how to look out for myself without turning my back on everyone else.
5. Have some fun for a change.

11 Now What?

On Saturday morning Jessica ate a bowl of Golden Grahams, then sat back at the kitchen table and stared at the doorway while she drank her orange juice. She was still angry with Elizabeth about last night and was all set to blast her as soon as she came downstairs. But for once Elizabeth, the up-and-at-'em go-getter, was sleeping in. It figured.

Luckily their parents had gone out to do some early errands this morning, and Jessica was taking advantage of having the place to herself. At least it gave her some time to sort out what she was going to say. She still couldn't believe that her sister had ruined her plans for some stupid internship.

Well, maybe not *ruined*. She had to admit that last night hadn't been so bad after all. Finding out Elizabeth wasn't coming had at least broken the ice with C. J., and by the time their food arrived, they had all kind of settled in as if nothing had happened. The five of them had even gone to the Riot

159

afterward, and she and Tia had taken turns dancing with C. J. Then they'd switched off—Tia with Jeremy and Jessica with Trent. And Trent, it turned out, was some dancer.

Yeah, if she was really honest with herself, Jessica had to admit she really had a good time last night after all. But still—that wasn't the point. The point was, Jessica didn't want her sister to keep blowing her off, and she wanted Elizabeth to understand that. She also would have liked her *boyfriend* to understand it. Frankly, it struck her as a little weird that Jeremy had acted like she was so far off base for being upset with Elizabeth. *Maybe it's just a guy thing,* she reasoned. But then why had Trent seemed to get it?

A few minutes later she heard Elizabeth's soft scuffing on the stairs, and then her sister walked into the kitchen, still in the shorts and T-shirt she had worn to bed and with a serious case of bed head.

When she saw Jessica sitting there, she froze. Jessica still wasn't sure what she wanted to say, so she looked down at the fashion magazine that was in her lap.

Elizabeth inched slowly toward her and put her hands on the table. "Jess," she said softly. "I am just so sorry about last night."

Jessica turned a page of the magazine and said nothing.

"Really," Elizabeth went on. "You have no idea. I . . . I just couldn't leave the office. Believe me, now I wish I had. But that's a whole other story."

Jessica looked up at her but still didn't say a word.

"You wouldn't believe what it was like," Elizabeth said. "Yesterday everyone was on deadline, and the place was just crazy. They had me doing all this really important research, and then they asked me to call and get quotes for—"

"That's nice, Liz. I'm glad you had fun." Jessica drained her glass of orange juice and banged it down on the table.

Elizabeth looked hurt. She stood upright and began to say something, but Jessica cut her off.

"Liz, you have no idea what you put me through last night. What you put everybody through."

"I . . . what do you mean?"

"I mean everyone went to a lot of trouble for you, and you just totally ruined it." She paused, then said, "Trent brought a date for you last night."

Elizabeth gasped. "*What?*" she cried.

"He was a really cute, sweet, funny guy that you would have totally been into. But now we'll be lucky to ever see him again because he was so completely humiliated at being stood up."

Elizabeth's hand slowly moved to cover her mouth. "But Jess, I didn't even know—"

161

"I know." Jessica's voice dropped a few notches now. "That's why I'm only *angry* at you right now instead of *furious*. But I knew you'd never come if you thought it was a fix up. You've been so crazed over this job. I just wanted to show you that there are other things in life besides work and school and . . . and work."

Elizabeth nodded, pressing her lips together. "You're right," she said. "There definitely are other things."

Jessica took a deep breath. She was still mad but trying to control it. "You seem to have forgotten that lately."

Elizabeth reached over and touched her sister's wrist. "Look," she said, "I've snapped out of it. Believe me."

Elizabeth squeezed Jessica's hand, and after a moment Jessica reluctantly squeezed her back. She had to admit she felt better now that she'd said all she had to say. Obviously Elizabeth was truly sorry, and it sounded like she'd had a pretty rough night.

"Okay," Jessica said. "So tell me about your night. How was it?"

Elizabeth groaned, but then blew her bangs out of her eyes and sat back hard in a chair. "Well, let's see. I worked my butt off and got zero credit for it because my supervisor told our boss *he* did it all."

Jessica's jaw dropped. *"What?"* she demanded.

Elizabeth shook her head. "I stayed late to contact some sources for Leo and get a bunch of new quotes. I got some great ones too. Then Joanna calls, and I overhear Leo telling her how much work he'd gotten done. Only it was *my work!*"

Jessica took that in for a moment, then exploded. "Are you *kidding* me?" she cried. "They're not even paying you! Oh my God, and those jerks ruined *my* night too! I can't believe this! I hope you told that guy off."

"I did," Elizabeth promised.

"Because if I'd been there," Jessica went on, "believe me, Leo would still be picking up the pieces of his shattered little ego by the time I'd finished with him—"

Elizabeth started to say something, but Jessica cut her off.

"Oh! I just had an idea! Do you want me to go down there and pretend to be you? I could totally scream at that guy because I bet you let him off easy—"

"No, Jess." Elizabeth held up her hand. "No."

"I'd be happy to do it."

Elizabeth laughed. "I *bet.*"

"What's so funny?" Jessica demanded.

"Does this mean I'm forgiven?" Elizabeth asked.

Jessica faked a frown but couldn't keep the smile from her face. "Oh, I guess," she said. "Just do me a favor."

"Anything. I'll go out with whoever you want."

Jessica rolled her eyes and smiled. "Let's put that on hold for now." Then she looked hard at Elizabeth, locking eyes with her twin, thinking of how the last few days had been almost scary, the way Elizabeth was behaving. "Just don't turn into someone like Leo, Liz," she said. "No matter how rough the job is."

Elizabeth went to the fridge and got her own glass of juice. "Don't worry. I know I've been really intense lately, but I think I've got my priorities back in order . . . finally." She started for the stairs, then turned back again and smiled at Jessica. "Thanks for getting all worked up about it, though. That was really sweet."

"Hey," Jessica said, "nobody treats my sister that way. Especially when they end up messing up *my* night too."

Elizabeth laughed and sprinted up the stairs.

Okay, maybe now things can get back to normal around here, Jessica thought. *Elizabeth knows she was wrong—she didn't even argue about it. And now there's only one other person who still needs to know that. And he's about to get a call.*

* * *

164

CNN had been on downstairs for a while—Ken could hear it even through his closed bedroom door. And that meant his father was up, sitting at the dining-room table and watching *Headline News* while he ate breakfast. Ken knew he had to get down there before his dad left for work, to tell him what he'd decided about the scholarship and get it over with. But he'd been thinking that since seven o'clock, and here he was, still in bed, staring at a crack in the ceiling.

Finally he swung himself out of bed, threw on yesterday's T-shirt and jeans, and headed downstairs. There was his dad, just as he'd pictured, sipping coffee from his favorite blue mug and staring at the tube. "Morning," he said to Ken, in that strained voice he'd used ever since their big blowup when Ken had first found out the truth.

"Hey," Ken replied. He went into the kitchen and slumped against the counter, watching his father through the doorway. His dad began buttering his toast, and Ken knew he was spreading the margarine in one thin layer from crust to crust—perfectly even all over—just like he'd always, always done.

His life is so ordered, Ken thought. *No surprises. No disruptions. Well, he's in for a big shock today.*

Ken gripped the edge of the counter, realizing his heart was starting to beat faster. Before he had a chance to completely flip out, he marched into the dining room and sat down beside his father.

It actually took his dad a minute to realize Ken was sitting beside him. Apparently the segment he was watching was pretty interesting. "Something on your mind?" he asked at last, turning to Ken and muting the television.

"Well—I—uh," Ken fumbled. He rubbed his hands briskly up and down his thighs, then simply blurted it out. "I gave up the scholarship," he said. Ken couldn't even bear to look at his father, so he just stared at the floor as he went on. "Dad, you have no idea what things have been like for me lately," he said softly. "I can't eat. Can't sleep. Can't study. All because I couldn't figure out what to do. And then, after that dinner the other night, I decided Garrett was pretty all right. I signed the letter, and then I called him. But I got someone else on the phone. He said Garrett's leaving next year. And I just felt—I just felt that I'd had enough *lies*, Dad."

He stopped to catch his breath. It was funny, but the more he talked, the calmer he felt and the more convinced he became of just how right he was to do what he did.

"So anyway," he finished, "it's a done deal. And . . . well, I just wanted you to know."

Now Ken sat still, staring at the silent TV, watching some news footage of a pro basketball game from yesterday. His dad remained quiet for so long that Ken finally forced himself to look at him. He was staring down at his plate.

Finally his father wiped his mouth with his napkin. "I guess that explains the mess I found in here yesterday," he said thickly.

Ken simply looked at him, having no idea what he was talking about.

"Michigan catalogs lying all over the floor? Or don't you remember?"

Suddenly it all clicked into place. *Oh, man, I just nearly gave myself a heart attack over that little speech . . . and my dad already knew? He must have figured it out when he saw the letter of intent in about a thousand pieces. But why didn't he say anything?* Ken looked sideways at his father. He looked tired. *I guess he wanted to hear it from me.* "Yeah," Ken said slowly. "I remember. Sorry. I meant to clean it up later."

"That's just the thing, isn't it, son?" his father said. "You make these messes and you go on your merry way and leave it to others to straighten things out behind you."

Ken shook his head. "No, Dad. I know what you're saying. And I'm sorry if I've screwed things up before. But not this time. This time I'm making the right decision. Whether you agree with it or not."

His father stared at him—that steely, penetrating

stare that always made Ken want to look away. But he wouldn't this time. Because he knew he was right.

Somehow it seemed to work. After a few seconds his father appeared to realize he wasn't going to win. Finally he broke the gaze, glanced at his plate again, and pushed his chair back from the table.

"Well, it's your life, Ken," he said, standing. "I guess you have to live it your way. I just have one question." He looked down at Ken, his face suddenly taking on a totally innocent, casual expression. "Now what?"

Ken stared at him. He was at a loss for words.

"That's what I thought," his father said, before leaving the room.

"Jess," Jeremy said, after hearing Jessica's hello. "I was just about to call you."

"Really?" Jessica asked. "I'm just glad I didn't wake you. We were out pretty late last night. . . ." *Okay, this is good. . . . We're talking about last night. Now I'll just ease the conversation to Elizabeth so I can explain why I was so mad. . . .*

"Speaking of last night . . ." Jeremy hesitated. When he spoke again, his voice was softer. "I wanted to say I'm sorry."

Jessica stared at the receiver. *What?*

"I mean, I think I was just uncomfortable," he went on. "I felt so bad for C. J. that I didn't want to make things worse by making a big deal about how mad we all were at Liz. Anyway, I think I just went overboard the other way. I was a little freaked out, I guess."

Jessica didn't know what to say. *So—wait a minute—is he actually taking my side?*

"Jess? You still there?"

"So—so you think I was right to be mad?" she asked.

"Yeah," he said. "I'm sorry if I made you feel like you weren't. And once we were there—I actually thought C. J. would have been good for Liz."

Jessica wrapped the phone cord around her finger. "Me too," she said finally. "Anyway, Liz apologized, so I'm over it. She's pretty upset, actually."

"That's good," Jeremy said, then caught himself. "I mean, not that she's upset, but, you know, that she apologized. And I apologize too. For making you feel worse when I should have made you feel better."

Okay, two apologies in one morning. That's enough for anybody.

"Well," Jessica admitted, "it *was* pretty awkward. I guess I should have thought it through more, like you said. And I definitely should have let Liz in on the whole thing. Even if I was afraid she wouldn't come if she knew."

"Okay," Jeremy said, "so let's just file last night under 'lessons learned' and forget about it."

Jessica thought for a minute. "Well, I don't know. Maybe we shouldn't forget about it totally. . . ."

"What do you mean?"

"We had a good time anyway, didn't we?" Jessica smiled, remembering little scenes from last night—hanging out and goofing around at the restaurant and then that dance with Trent.

"Yeah," Jeremy agreed warmly, "it was great. We should definitely hang out with Trent and Tia more often."

Jessica was startled by how glad she was to hear those words. "You read my mind," she said. "In fact, what do you think they're doing tonight?"

She heard a few seconds of silence on the phone. "I was hoping maybe tonight could be just the two of us," Jeremy said. "I mean, I definitely want to hang with them again soon, but I feel like we've hardly been alone at all lately." He paused, then said, "I guess I'm trying to say I miss you, okay?"

Jessica smiled into the receiver. Who'd have thought Jeremy could be such a romantic? "You miss me, huh?" she said. "Well, I can definitely fix that."

"So I'll see you around seven?" he asked.

"Great. I'll be watching for you."

After they said their good-byes, Jessica gazed at

the phone for a few moments, surprised to realize she still felt a bit disappointed. *Well, we can't do double dates* every *night,* she reasoned. And Tia and Trent probably wanted some time alone too.

But maybe next weekend . . .

Elizabeth tightened the belt of her thick terrycloth bathrobe and flopped onto her bed. She'd been putting off Maria's call as long as possible. She'd been a horrible friend, and now she had to "fess up," as her dad always said. Her hair was still wet from her shower, and she combed her fingers through it while she dialed the phone.

Maria answered with a sleepy-sounding hello.

"Late night or something?" Elizabeth teased.

"Oh, hey, Liz," she said. "Yeah. Ken and I were up late studying."

"Oh, *please.*" Elizabeth gave a little snort. "On a Friday night? Nice try."

Maria giggled. "Yeah," she said. "He's so great. First we did French and then this stupid sociology project I've been putting off."

Elizabeth's eyebrows flew up. *Is she serious?* "You've never sounded so happy about schoolwork."

"Well, let's just say that everything looks brighter today."

Elizabeth tightened her grip on the receiver.

"Does this mean that Ken's made his decision?"

"Yep. He's not going."

Elizabeth gasped. "You're kidding." But in an instant her surprise gave way to happiness. In fact, she felt better than she had in days. "That's great!"

"You have no idea *how* great," Maria said. "Ken found out that the Michigan coach won't be coming back next year—that both he and the scout had basically been lying about it. So that was just the last straw."

What a relief. Not only would she have been the worst friend in the world for turning in that proposal, but she'd have been dead wrong too! Mainly Elizabeth was really glad to hear that Ken was doing the right thing.

"I just wanted to say thanks," Maria said, "for being a great friend and for keeping Ken's secret. I know that wasn't an easy thing to do."

Elizabeth stared at the receiver. Now Maria had to be kidding. Supportive? Elizabeth had been totally absorbed in herself! Should she tell her "great friend" how she'd almost spilled Ken's secret—and to the whole town, no less? The thought made her cringe. "Maria, I—"

"Listen, Liz, I'm sorry, but Mom's got to use the phone. I'll call you later, okay?"

Elizabeth hesitated but finally said, "Sure," and

hung up. She stared down at her pillow and twirled a piece of her hair. She hadn't had a chance to "fess up" to Maria after all, but maybe it was for the best. After all, she *had* kept Ken's secret. Even if fate had to intervene to *make* her keep it.

She stood up and looked in the mirror above her dresser as she ran a comb through her damp hair. She thought about how much older she always looked when her hair was wet. *Well, I am older, aren't I?* she realized. *Old enough to stand up for myself, at least.* Elizabeth gazed at her reflection, realizing she couldn't let herself be scared off—not from a job she loved so much. She just had to watch her back. There was nothing wrong with learning that skill either. And she didn't have to make this job her life. From now on, friends and family would always come first.

She grinned at herself, knowing that putting others first meant she would be slipping back into "old Elizabeth"—the one she'd been trying to ditch all along. But who cared? She was who she was. And what was so bad about that?

KEN MATTHEWS
1:32 P.M.

If you'd asked me how I felt last night, I'd have told you fantastic. Relieved. Totally chilled. Like I've been carrying around this giant rock for the past few weeks and now I'm finally able to drop it. Maria was right—everything did work out in the end. And even that talk with my dad wasn't nearly as bad as it could have been.

There's just that one little problem to deal with, the one Dad asked me about. I mean, it's not like I haven't thought about it at all—just not as much as I probably should have by now. Those two simple little words that pretty much mean everything.

Now what?

Time to pick that rock right back up— and maybe just start banging my head against it.

JEREMY AAMES
2:43 P.M.

I can't believe how great things have worked out lately. Jessica and I are totally clicking, and now here's Trent and Tia like two goopy lovebirds or something—just what I'd hoped would happen to Trent. It's almost like it's too good to be true. And you know what the best part is? It's that we all get along so great and do such cool stuff together. Hey, if it were up to Jessica, we'd be doing the foursome thing every night. Anyway, this is definitely a good thing.

What could be bad about it?

TIA RAMIREZ
3:54 P.M.

WHY DO I HAVE TO WORRY
ABOUT THE STUPIDEST THINGS?
WHY CAN'T I JUST ENJOY LIFE AND
WALK AROUND WITH MY HEAD IN
THE CLOUDS LIKE MOST PEOPLE?
WELL, OKAY, SO MAYBE I THINK TOO
MUCH—JUMP TO THE WRONG
CONCLUSIONS. BUT IT SEEMS LIKE
EVEN SOMEONE WITH HER HEAD
ABOVE THE STRATOSPHERE WOULD
NOTICE THE WAY JESSICA AND TRENT
HAVE BEEN ACTING. CALL ME CRAZY,
BUT AREN'T THEY CONSTANTLY
STICKING UP FOR EACH OTHER AND
AGREEING WITH EACH OTHER AND
COMING UP WITH ALL THESE LITTLE
PLANS TOGETHER? IS IT JUST MY
IMAGINATION? TELL ME IT IS.

CALL ME CRAZY—_PLEASE!_

CONNER MCDERMOTT

4:30 P.M.

I should call Alanna. I have to call her. But maybe I can just wait until after the weekend. I need a little more time to think everything through. Next week. I'll call her next week.

ALANNA FELDMAN

4:43 P.M.

If I don't hear from Conner by tomorrow morning, I'm calling him. And I won't stop calling until he gets on the phone. I'm tired of being avoided, and it's about to stop.